Kurt followed his dog, Matilda, as she led him to the steps of the airy, wooden front porch of his new home.

Just then the door swung open, and there was April Shelnutt. If not the very person he'd come out here to escape, she was the personification of his problem. He stood frozen on the spot, before finally asking, "What are you doing here?"

She tilted her head, and soft wisps of hair drifted against the side of her neck. It made him think of the way her hair fell in glossy waves when she didn't wear it in a braid. And of how soft that hair felt between his work-roughened fingers. And of how good she smelled... All of which reminded him why he'd gone to great pains to avoid her—to avoid noticing things like that about her.

And now she was standing in his doorway.

Books by Annie Jones

Love Inspired

April in Bloom #343

Steeple Hill Café

Sadie-in-Waiting
Mom Over Miami

ANNIE JONES,

winner of the Holt Medallion for Southern Themed
Fiction, and the *Houston Chronicle*'s Best Christian
Fiction Author of 1999, grew up in a family that
loved to laugh, eat and talk—often all at the same
time. They instilled in her the gift of sharing through
words and humor, and the confidence to go after her
heart's desire (and to act fast if she wanted the last
chicken leg). A former social worker, she feels called
to be a "voice for the voiceless" and has carried that
calling into her writing by creating characters often
overlooked in our fast-paced culture—from seventy-
somethings who still have a zest for life to women
over thirty with big mouths and hearts to match.
Having moved thirteen times during her marriage,
she is currently living in rural Kentucky with her
husband and two children.

APRIL IN BLOOM
ANNIE JONES

Steeple
Hill®

Published by Steeple Hill Books™

STEEPLE HILL BOOKS

Steeple
Hill®

ISBN 0-373-87361-1

APRIL IN BLOOM

The Lord will guide you always;
He will satisfy your needs in a sun-scorched land
and will strengthen your frame.
You will be like a well-watered garden,
like a spring whose waters never fail.
—*Isaiah* 58:11

Chapter One

"Rootbound, Sheriff Muldoon. That's your problem." The spry old fellow standing in the open doorway swept the gray felt hat from his head, sucked his teeth and squinted hard. "Got no room to grow. And if you don't do something about it and quick, well, I ain't one to be a prophet of doom, but if you don't make a change soon, there'll be no hope at all."

Kurt shuddered as if a cold wind had overtaken him. The portent of a coming storm.

"Come on in, Moonie." He tried to sound gruff. Amused but gruff. "Tell me what's on your mind—not like I could stop you from it."

Unstoppable. Somebody would be hard-pressed to find a soul in Wileyville, Kentucky, who would argue with that description of Solomon "Moonie" Shelnutt.

The older gentleman took a few steps inside the sheriff's stuffy office and jabbed one gnarled finger at the potted plant bullied into a windowless corner beside cardboard boxes and outdated computer equipment. "That plant."

"What plant?" Kurt pivoted in his squeaky chair to eye the thin-stalked palm, its fringed leaves tinged with brown.

"That one." This time, Moonie motioned with his familiar hat. "Needs room to spread out. To stretch and grow and realize its full potential. Never going to happen if you keep it confined to this place."

Kurt blinked to ease the ever-present burning in his eyes from the flickering fluorescent lights overhead and sighed. "I know just how it feels."

"I'll get my daughter April to come 'round and look after it for you, if you want." April, Moonie's stepdaughter, was hardly a girl but to the man who had raised her and done everything possible to keep her and her sisters with him even after their mother abandoned them, she would always be his "girl". Kurt respected and admired that even if the old man's suggestion made him cringe.

"No!" It startled even Kurt how sharp his refusal came out. But any contact between him and April Shelnutt was something he could not encourage in good conscience.

Not with April. Not now. Not ever.

Not that there was anything wrong with the independent, unpretentious woman with the golden-brown braid and smile that could light a man's way out of the darkest despair.

He rubbed his forehead, as if that action could erase her image from his mind. Not that it mattered. Even if he succeeded in ridding himself of the memory of her face, the feelings she evoked in him would always remain deep within him. And that was where they had to stay. Deep within. For both of their sakes.

If it didn't hurt so much, it would be funny. The irony of it all. After so many years for both of them to finally find each other, only to meet in a time and place…

Impossible. It simply could not be. That part of Kurt's life was dead and over.

April Shelnutt was the one woman he could have finally chosen to make a life with. Problem was, she was the kind of woman who wanted a *real* life—marriage, a home and everything that went with it. Right out in the open where people could stick their big, fat noses in and start with what they'd call advice or, worse, support. Yes, they would be well-intentioned. Well, *most* of them would be but in the end, the result would be the same. Kurt would end up hurt and hurting the people he loved, those who should have trusted him most.

He could not let that happen. Not again. Not to April Shelnutt.

That was why he insisted that if they were to see each other, the relationship had to remain on his terms. For a while, April had gone along with his intense need for privacy. They had met in secret. Taken separate cars to "run into each other" at out-of-town restaurants. They never acknowledged each other much in public.

"Fine afternoon, huh, Sheriff?" she would murmur in passing.

"Yes, ma'am." He'd tip his hat and, in the shadow of the brim, sneak in a smile and sometimes a wink.

She'd walk away with an extra spring in her step.

He knew because he'd watch her in the side mirror of his county car.

If Kurt had his way, none of that would have changed.

But April's life had changed, and with it came the need to do what Moonie prescribed for the palm in the corner. She needed to stretch and grow, to break free of the confines of her old ways and find new directions that would allow her, at long last, to blossom.

Kurt couldn't blame her. He, of all people, understood the roles that loss and self-examination played in shaping life choices. The death of his wife, Carol, had certainly determined how he would live out the remainder of his days.

As an ex-army officer, the town's sheriff and a man of honor and faith, what choice did he have really?

He had to do the right thing for April, even if it was the worst thing for him. He had to stay as far away from her as possible.

"Don't bother your daughter on my behalf, Moonie. It's, uh—" he gazed at the sad specimen struggling to survive out of its element—not unlike a certain career army man who had plunked down in his old hometown without any real sense of purpose "—it's just a plant."

"She won't mind. Got a servant's heart, that one. Good girl. Fix you right up, she would."

Kurt didn't doubt April's abilities for a moment. And being reminded of her again and again made him all the more terse when he wheeled his chair around and rested his forearms on the edge of his desk. "You sure you're in the right office, Moonie?"

The lines in the man's face deepened. His bushy white eyebrows inched downward. "What?"

"Well, if you've come to discuss agriculture, you want the county agent's office, not mine."

"Agriculture? No, sir." He laughed. *"Aggravation.* That's what's on my agenda for today."

"Well, at least you're up-front and honest about it." Which was more than Kurt could say about a lot of people around town. "What is it you've come to aggravate me about today?"

"Me? I'll have you know, I ain't aggravated a soul in—"

Kurt cleared his throat.

"Hours," Moonie finished, a slow, sly grin working across his face. "But seriously, son, I didn't come here to vex you none. I came to warn you."

Not what Kurt had hoped to hear. He edged forward, his eyes keenly trained on the man. "Warn me? About what?"

"That meddling bunch of the COCW, that's what."

"The Council of Christian Women?" Kurt didn't know whether to laugh or grumble under his breath. Either way he'd regret it. He didn't want to hurt the old man's feelings or break his commitment as a man of God and a town role model to keep his language clean. "What's the matter, Moonie? That wild gang of ministers' wives, church ladies and vigilante prayer warriors up to no good again?"

The man narrowed his eyes. "Worse."

"Worse?"

"Instead of being up to *no* good, they are up to *some* good. And I have to tell you, that's when their kind becomes most dangerous!"

"Up to what?"

"Guess you ain't heard about the project then?"

"Project?"

"Yup. To mark this time leading up to Easter." He nodded toward the calendar. "You know how some folks give something up at this time of year?"

"Sure."

"Well, this crowd has got it in their collective fancy, hairdo-ed heads that them that don't practice the service of sacrifice should go over and above and out of their way to do more, to give something back."

"Back?"

"To the community. To the churches. Whoever they deem needs it."

"Needs what?"

"Well, *that's* the rub, ain't it? The *what!*"

Kurt squeezed his eyes shut and scoured his forehead with callused fingers. "Moonie, you do realize I am armed and cranky?"

"Meaning?"

Kurt grinned, just enough to keep things friendly, then slammed his fist on the desk hard enough to make his nameplate clatter but gently enough to avoid starting an avalanche of the piled-high files. "Get to the point, man!"

"Okay, here it is." Moonie leaned forward and, twisting the brim of his hat ever so slightly, whispered, "Watch your back."

"My back?"

"And your front, for that matter. I know these women. They're tricky. They could be coming at you from all directions."

The image of silver-haired ladies in floral dresses and combat boots crouched around every corner of Wileyville popped into Kurt's head. He laughed. "I've been trained in hand-to-hand combat, heavy artillery and personal firearms. I think I can fend off a pack of church ladies."

Moonie shook his head. "You just don't get it, boy."

"What's to get? The nice Christian ladies want people to be kinder to one another for a few weeks. I say, let them go for it." He pushed his hand through his hair and suddenly recalled his mother's admonition not to do that, as it tended to make the gray in his usually nondescript light-brown hair stand out.

"You've had such handsome brown hair your whole life and now you move home and suddenly you go gray," his mother, who had gone white-headed at a young age herself, had tsked him. "What will people say?"

What people would say mattered to Kurt's mother. A lot. And why wouldn't it? When you are the town's biggest gossip, you have a unique vantage point from which to understand just how vicious and vulgar rumors and idle chatter can be.

"Anyway, I don't see how anything the COCW does applies to me. I don't have a home church these days." And he wasn't looking for one. Talk about a way to open yourself up to people—no way. "I think of myself more as a free-range Christian."

"Don't matter. Churched or unchurched, if they take a notion to throw down a good deed on a person, they'll do 'er and they'll do 'er big time." Moonie wagged a finger. "And don't kid yourself, Sheriff. You are just one great big good deed waiting to happen. They have plans for you. Mark my words."

Kurt shook his head again, chuckled under his breath and feigned a sudden all-enthralling interest in the disheveled file spread open before him. "I'm not worried, Moonie."

"Well, you should be." The man squashed his hat down low on his head, moved to the door, then turned, the usual mischief in his eyes honed to steely solemnity. "There is no more fearsome force on God's green earth than righteous women with a cause. They have rallied against hunger, poverty, ignorance and injustice. They have brought down despots, altered the course of history and changed the very fabric of entire cultures. They are fearless in taking on any and all things that offend them."

Kurt's shoulders tensed. "And?"

"And few things offend them more than a happy bachelor."

Kurt sat up straight as a rod. His chair gave a weak squawk under the shift in his weight.

"Mark my words, son. You are in their sights, and when God-fearing, home-loving, matchmaking females get a man in their sights... Well, just remember, women like that have married off more determinedly single men than you."

Chapter Two

"Nobody likes me, everybody hates me, I'm going out in the garden and eat worms."

"Big, fat, juicy ones. Itty-bitty, slimy ones…" April stabbed the tip of her gardener's trowel into the dark, rich ground and, without even twisting around to look over her shoulder, called out, "Hello, Miss Cora."

Miss Cora Barrett. That was all she needed.

April spent her weekdays running the Weed 'Em and Reap Garden Supply and Nursery. Over the past decade or so, she'd set aside a couple of evenings a week for dinner with her sisters and their families, school plays, recitals or church youth-group fund-raisers for her niece and nephew. And trying to keep one step ahead of her darling daddy was one of those on-call 24/7 deals. That left Sundays after church her only time to let off steam. And today, she had built up enough steam, courtesy of a certain impossible-to-pin-down sheriff, to run the town's power plant for a week. She needed a way to blow off some of that pent-up energy.

Pent-up energy. Nice-girl talk for getting angry.

Nice girls, you see, don't get angry. Agitated, perhaps. Peeved. Exasperated. Nice girls worked themselves into a tizzy. And if they were of a certain kind—pampered, of high social standing or deemed by good folks as "high-strung," nice girls might just find themselves inclined from time to time to throw an outright, huffing-and-puffing, flouncing-and-object-flingin' hissy fit. But they did not get angry. They especially did not harbor anger.

If April was anything, she was a nice girl.

Or was she a *good* girl?

All right. She was a patsy. First-class.

When it came right down to it, that was what she had become, and everyone knew it. One man most of all, and clearly even little Miss Cora saw it. Saw it and hoped to take advantage of it by honing in on April's only time to herself, her only time to work in the garden.

Garden? She sat back on her heels and gazed at the four-by-ten-foot strip of median in the parking lot behind the 80-year-old building that housed both her growing business and her cramped apartment. Still, to April, it was an oasis. Her retreat from the world. An escape from the demands of others. Her chance to plant, to cultivate, to nurture a little something that made her and her alone happy.

And now that retreat had been encroached upon by someone who had not *just* come by to chat or to fill a few empty hours. Not Miss Cora. The old gal wanted something, and she wanted it from April now.

And being a good girl—okay, *patsy*—April had to at least hear the woman out.

"Let's all go eat worms!" Miss Cora completed the children's song with boisterous joy. Well, as boisterous as a birdlike ninety-year-old dolled up in her Sunday best could get.

April ran her hand back over her hair, realizing too late that she'd probably left a streak of dirt from her forehead to the first plaits of her freshly done braid. She sighed. Did it really matter? She could go around with a robin's nest on her head and who would really notice? No one ever looked at her. "You feeling better today, Miss Cora? I heard you had a cold."

"Oh, you know me. To keep me down, something would have to put up with me and, so far, nobody's been able to do that for very long."

April smiled.

"*You* know how that is." Miss Cora reached down and nudged her shoulder.

She did know. But that didn't keep her from getting riled up at the suggestion. Sure, plenty of folks around town had made that same comparison between the women, even though April was not even half her age. April and Miss Cora, the town's resident old maids.

Hardly flattering, even if the townsfolk looked kindly on both women as spinsters with sass in their tongues, starch in their backbones, and hearts… Hearts that should have held the love of a husband and children but, for some reason, never received that blessing.

Yet, April reminded herself. She wasn't giving up entirely. Not yet. She was only giving up on one man. And one man was not the be-all and end-all of her romantic potential. He was just…

"Now listen here, Miss Cora." April threw back her shoulders and angled up her chin. "It is one thing to admit you're too ornery to take up with a virus, but don't go lumping me in with you."

"Take up with a virus!" Miss Cora let loose something between a giggle and a snort. "I reckon I had a beau or two that fit that description in my day. How 'bout you?"

April's last official called-a-week-ahead, came-up-to-the-front-door, took-her-out-to-eat-in-public-and-at-least-offered-to-pay-for-her-meal—though didn't-ask-twice-when-she-suggested-they-split-the-bill—date flashed through her mind. She chuckled. Ruefully.

And then there was…*him*. April clenched her

teeth. "I confess, Miss Cora, there have been a few fellows in my life that, given the choice between spending another evening with them and a week with your virus, I'd take your virus in place of."

"Still, better to have courted a germ and lost than to have stayed healthy and never been courted at all." Miss Cora folded her hands, tilted her head and sighed. "Right, girl?"

"I—I suppose so." To say her reply lacked enthusiasm was a gross understatement. "Though, like viruses, some of those germs take a lot more time to get over than others, and until you are over them, well, it's hard not to wish you'd avoided them altogether."

"What doesn't kill us makes us stronger," Cora said in such a way that April knew the old gal had experienced that adage and believed it with all her fragile old heart.

There are women who do not ache for love, marriage, home and family. Some live amazing, adventurous, even awe-inspiring lives. Full lives. So full, they don't seem to have room for loneliness or regrets. Cora and April were not that kind of woman, and everyone who knew them knew it.

Heart on her sleeve? April wore it like a merit badge on a sash across her chest. Though she tried to shield it, to guard herself always as the verse her father had chosen for her as a child—Ephesians 6:13—said: "Therefore, take unto you the whole armor of God, that ye may be able to withstand in the evil day and, having done all, to stand."

April had stood against silence and sorrow in her family. She had stood against disappointment and dissatisfaction in her personal life. She had prayed, hoped and waited. And then, at last, after so many years of doing everything just the way she was told she was supposed to, she met a man with humor in his green eyes and a winning smile meant only for her.

She thought Kurt Muldoon was The One.

And he was. The one who made her feel like a big, sappy, plain-Jane, middle-aged fool.

A surge of that nice-girl pent-up energy made the hair prickle on her arms and the back of her neck. Heat rose from her chest to her face. Her stomach knotted.

He'd taken up her time, poked holes in her vanity, forced her to take stock of her life. And that was okay. That she'd survived when it all fell apart. But he'd played her for a fool and left her the object of pity. That was something she could not, would not brook.

What's more, he'd made her simple but most profound hopes seem foolish and had exploited her greatest vulnerability and weaknesses. Ouch. She shut her eyes tight against the harshness of the very thought. Her own weaknesses and vulnerability.

April did not know if she could ever forgive him. But as a Christian, she would. She would have to find a way. But she did not *want* to do it.

Which only made her more pent-up. With herself.

April sat on the ground and looked up at her visitor.

Wonderful, wild-eyed, well-intentioned Miss Cora. Ninety years young and no bigger than a spring sapling, the white-haired fireball had been a mainstay of Wileyville town culture since... since, well, almost since the founding of Wileyville itself.

Her family, the Barretts, along with the Fursts and the Bartletts, had founded the town. There was a story there. The one thing the families agreed upon was naming the town for a mutual ancestor. Beyond that they argued over every detail. So much so that at one meeting over how to divvy up what would become the downtown area three ways, a knife was drawn. No, no bloodshed ensued. But the map got sliced up and the town forever after had two main streets running north and south, a third at the top and a point near what later became the cemetery, making it look forevermore like a piece of pie.

April knew the tale by heart, just as she knew why Miss Cora had come by today and what the old dear wanted.

At that reminder, she gripped the handle of the gardening tool in her gloved hand and dragged the tip of the trowel over the still-hard ground.

"Why so glum, darlin'?"

April punched the blade deep into the ground,

then began to work it loose again. The comforting smell of damp soil filled her nostrils. "I'm not glum. I'm...introspective."

"Don't kid me, young lady. I know you. Known you since you were a babe in arms and your parents before you. Taught them in Sunday school, just like most everyone in this town."

"Miss Cora, my parents grew up in Tennessee." *Ping.* The tip of her trowel hit a rock. She clenched her jaw. "My father moved me and my sisters here when we were little."

"That right?"

Right? April pondered. Well, it was *true.*

She'd recently come to question how right the choice had been. After years of keeping his silence—and, by example and by subtle exhortation, encouraging April to do the same—her father had finally revealed the reasons behind their exodus from Tennessee. In doing so, he had rocked the very foundations of April's role in the family.

She kept her jaw clenched to try to force down the panic rising in her throat. Her weaknesses. Her vulnerability.

For almost forty years, April had been the keeper of family secrets. She and the Lord alone had known the story. And she had kept it between them. She had to or risk tearing her family apart forever.

Only the secret *did* come out. Those kinds of things usually do, even if they take a lifetime to surface. But the family had not come apart. If anything, they had grown closer.

Much as she cherished that outcome, April couldn't help wondering if the sacrifices she made had all been for nothing. She had not lived a noble existence—she had lived a lie.

At their mother's grave, her sisters had finally been able to heal the wounds of a lifetime spent wondering why they had been abandoned, and with that visit, they put the past where it belonged: behind them. But where did that leave April? Where did *she* belong?

April stared down at her unremarkable plot of land. *Where did she belong?*

"So you're not from here?" Disbelief tinged the old woman's tone, as if maybe it was April who suffered lapses in memory and not herself. "Your mama nor your daddy, either?"

"No, Miss Cora. My mother never lived here." Because of untreated depression, her mother hadn't *lived* much of anywhere. Her life had been that devastated. And to keep the disease from doing the same to her three daughters, she had sent them away and broken all ties. April alone held any memories of their mother. Faint memories. Or were they dreams or things she'd only imagined? Moonie had forbidden them to talk about that chapter of their past so April had held them inside, guarding them and protecting her sisters from her darkest suspicions.

"Daddy moved Sadie, Hannah and me here when they were tiny and I was about six."

"That so?" Miss Cora folded her arms over her pink cotton dress, which hiked up enough to show another layer of lace from her perpetually sagging petticoat. "Who is your daddy, child?"

April sat back, resting on the heels of her hiking boots, and finally looked the old gal in the eye. "Moonie Shelnutt."

"Oh, of course! I knew that." The pale paper-thin skin around Miss Cora's eyes crinkled. She blinked, looking at nothing in particular, and frowned. "Surely, I knew that."

At her age, Miss Cora had forgotten more things than April ever knew. But there was one thing she had not forgotten—one thing she would never forget or ever let go of...

"But I didn't come 'round to talk about your daddy. I came by to ask—"

"When am I going to take you out to Ezra's Holler?"

Tucked into a place so remote that one had to stand at the opening and "holler" to announce one's self before venturing in, Ezra's Holler was Miss Cora's home. Three generations of Barretts had called it home, for that matter, and with Miss Cora being the last of the lot still living in the area, it remained her personal domain in the minds of the longtime locals.

Roughly a hundred years ago, Miss Cora's grandfather—the Reverend Ezra Barrett—had staked out the untouched land, etched through by a craggy creek feeding into a small lake, as the setting for a new town. A moral town. A town that would serve the Lord. A town that, despite having a church, a jail, a school and some houses, never really came to fruition.

The remoteness of Ezra's Holler had worked against it. The type of people drawn to such a place rarely were interested in obeying ordinances, electing town officials and paying city taxes. Ezra, whom many people accused of preaching to the choir because he rarely interacted with anyone outside the church, couldn't even piece together a gospel quartet in the holler that bore his name.

Now the town was just a collection of vacation cabins owned by absentee families, empty buildings and the once-grand old Barrett home. Miss Cora had finally moved away from the homestead seven years ago. She rented it to a family who had had enough of the isolation and constant upkeep six months ago and had moved to Wileyville. Now the place sat empty and neglected.

"I hate to burden you, sweet thing, but you did promise."

April drew in a breath and held it. The woman had her there. She *had* promised.

Five months ago.

That was when Miss Cora had wandered into the shop, agitated and confused and demanding. Why, she wanted to know, hadn't April sent any prizewinning tomato plants out to the house?

April told Miss Cora that she'd never sent *any* tomatoes to her, prizewinning or otherwise. Miss Cora, for want of a better term, begged to differ. Loudly. Using her cane to emphasize her point, alternately pounding the tip on the floor, waving it around and knocking knickknacks off the shelves in an attempt to swat April across the backside for sassing her elder.

One thing had led to another—or, more accurately, one thing had careened into another—and suddenly April had volunteered to take Miss Cora out to Ezra's Holler to check on the state of the garden.

"I promised to take you, but we agreed to wait until the weather and your health were better."

"It's a fine day today." Miss Cora held her hand out, palm up, then curled her knobby fingers into a trembling fist. One eye squinted closed and she grinned a gummy grin, then hunched her shoulders and gave a little cackle. "And as for me, I feel as spry as an eighty-year-old filled to the gills with spring tonic."

"Well, I have to admit, that's better than I feel some days." April laughed. "But taking you out to the holler, Miss Cora, is an event. Something I'm not sure *I'm* up to today."

"Nonsense. You're still a young woman." Miss Cora batted her hand in the air. "You could do this for me. I know it. I'm counting on it because—because I'm afraid I'm running out of time."

Guilt. Guilt. Guilt.

Why shouldn't Miss Cora pile it on?

Everyone else did.

And that was why it wasn't going to work.

Thanks to a lifetime of bearing far too much remorse over the loss of her mother and the way Kurt had encouraged her guarded nature to keep their relationship quiet, April was now immune to guilt.

"Now, Miss Cora, don't talk like that. Aren't you the one who says not to worry about how little time we have on earth but to rejoice in how long we have to serve God?"

"Lands, child, I don't mean I'm going to keel over dead! I plan to live that one hundred twenty-six years I heard of in the Bible."

April swept her gaze from the pink pillbox balanced delicately atop Miss Cora's thin puffs of white hair to her stick legs hidden under loose, opaque support hose to her wide feet in sturdy nurses' shoes. "I don't doubt it for one moment. So what's this about not having much time?"

"Didn't you hear?"

April pushed a stray strand of hair from her forehead and flipped her braid over her shoulder. "Hear what?"

"I sold the place."

"Sold?" She jerked her head up. "Ezra's Holler?"

"No. Not the whole holler. I don't own all that property anymore, you know. But I did sell what belonged to me. The school, the jail and the house—fully furnished, 'cept a few personal items."

Miss Cora selling her home? It seemed so…so final.

"Oh, Miss Cora, I had no idea."

Cora shrugged. "Couldn't be helped. Ain't cheap to grow old, girl."

"No." She laughed, but deep down, she couldn't shake an odd sense of loss over Miss Cora's choice. "I guess not."

"No use hanging on to something that no longer serves me and my walk in the Lord." She placed her hand on her hat and adjusted it with a jiggle that actually left the pillbox listing precariously to one side. "I teach Bible classes at the home now, you know."

"Um, yes, I did know that."

"Well, if I want to keep on going with that, I've got to be able to pay my bills. I still got another twenty-some years of them ahead, you know." She wagged her finger. "But I do so hope to go out to the old homestead soon. I want to make sure I haven't left anything precious behind."

Ezra's Holler was fifteen miles or so beyond Wileyville's town limits. That was all. A short drive for April, but it might as well have been the chasm between heaven and earth as far as Miss Cora was concerned.

Guilt. Guilt. Guilt.

April drew her shoulders up, her back as rigid as her resolve. Miss Cora had no idea who she was trying to guilt into doing her bidding. "I have plans right now, Miss Cora. Maybe we can look at my calendar and pick a day that suits both of us. Oh, and give us time to make sure it's all right with the new owner, of course."

Miss Cora gave her frail shoulders an empowering shimmy and pursed her lips. "That handsome young sheriff told me I could go on out there anytime I wanted to collect my personal things."

"Sheriff?" April's posture crumpled, if only slightly. She could scarcely believe what she'd heard. "*Our* sheriff?"

"I believe so."

"Kurt?" April blinked. *"Kurt Muldoon?* He bought a house? A great…big…*family* home? Are you sure you don't mean the deputy or the chief of police or, I don't know, someone else in a uniform? Uh, army recruiter? UPS man?"

"No. No one like that. The sheriff."

"Lollie Muldoon's son?"

"Yes. That's him." Cora gave a crisp nod that made her hat bobble. "Lollie's firstborn. Signed the papers last week. Says he won't be moving in right away, though."

"Why not? Once he's made up his mind about

something, he's pretty firm about it." And she should know. "Hesitating over a choice in life—even a blatantly misguided and shortsighted one—hardly sounds like Kurt."

"Misguided and shortsighted? No, honey, he knows where the house is, and best I can tell, his eyesight is fine. Why, it better be! They let him have a gun, you know."

"Miss Cora, I only meant—"

"Did you know that when I was growing up out there in the holler, *I* had a gun? And I knew how to use 'er, too." She held her finger up and closed one eye as if she was sighting down the barrel. "Can't raise a girl in the wilderness without her knowing how to protect herself, especially in a holler, where you might have to sometimes house fugitives from justice and ward off liniment salesmen."

"Yes, I'm sure that... Liniment salesmen?" April had to take a second to enjoy the image of tiny Miss Cora cradling a shotgun to ward off some poor unsuspecting ointment peddler. "Um, anyway, we were...that is, *you* were telling me that Kurt didn't plan to move into the house right away?"

"Wanted to take his things out there slowly, over time, so as not to draw attention to where he's going to. Got the feeling he wanted to keep things real hush-hush."

"Ah." She nodded, putting the pieces together at last. "*That* sounds like him."

"Said he wouldn't move out there full-time till he'd finished up a few things in town."

"Finished up? In town?" What could that mean? She didn't dare sit and speculate for fear she'd convince herself it had something—everything—to do with her. Intellectually, she knew it didn't. But her battered heart? It really did want to believe.

"I don't blame you if you'd rather not carry me out there." Miss Cora sighed.

"It's not that I don't want to carry you, Miss Cora." April rarely if ever used the term *carry* to refer to taking someone where they needed to go, but she wanted her elderly friend to know that she was listening and understood what was being asked. Even if she had no intention of driving to Ezra's Holler today. "It's just that I had my Sunday afternoon plans all laid out."

And if I go out to the home that Kurt has bought, it will only give me hope. False hope. No, thank you.

"I know, I know. Don't think I haven't been where you are now. You give so much of yourself—your time, your energy—and you don't mind. Really you don't."

"I—" April cleared her throat and glanced around the sunlit back street "—I don't. Really."

"But before long, everyone comes to expect it."

"Isn't that the truth?" April looked toward the cemetery where her sister worked as a superintendent. Sadie often asked April over to look at this flower or that shrub or give advice on dealing with grubs or gophers or possible grave robbers.

"Everybody thinks the single lady has nothing but time on her hands and surely she won't mind doing me this one teensy favor."

April turned to look over her shoulder toward the house where her daddy lived—and expected her to stop in daily to see him. "I hear that."

"Many is the time I'd want to just scurry under my bed, cover my head and shout to the next person who asked for something, 'Why don't you do it yourself?'"

"I know." April tapped the trowel blade against the curb to knock the bits of dirt from it. She couldn't look in any direction in this town and not be staring at a place that spelled commitment and obligation to her.

"And then one day, they did."

"Hmm?" April focused on Miss Cora again. "Did what?"

"Did it themselves."

"Oh."

"Not all at once, mind you. It was a slow thing. Children grew up. People moved away. Things changed."

The oldest of April's four nieces and nephews had gone off to college. Her youngest sister, Hannah, had moved with her hubby and children to Loveland, Ohio. Sadie had embarked on a new stage in her life, and Daddy… Well, Moonie did everything himself. Authentic independence, he liked to call it.

Sheer, stubborn orneriness, everyone else said.

Either way, the result was the same.

"After a while, you don't seem to fit in anywhere anymore," April murmured.

If Miss Cora heard her, she gave no indication—just stood there staring off into the distance, her hands folded and her hat askew. "All that time wasted rattling around that big old house when I might have been making more of my life, helping others, thinking about someone other than me and my puny existence."

April shifted the trowel from one hand to the other and, in doing so, caught a glimpse of her reflection and Miss Cora's.

She drew her breath in. Was she looking at her future?

She had felt her place in her familiar world begin to shift. First, in the monumental earthshaking way it did when they learned the truth about her mother's depression, and now in little aftershocks—her sisters' lives taking bold new directions, the man she thought might become her husband being unable to commit to even being seen as her sweetheart.

She supposed she could stay here and contemplate it all, withdraw into herself. Just as Miss Cora had all those years out at Ezra's Holler. Or she could get up and *do* something more with her life.

Kurt had made a move. Literally, figuratively, emotionally and…and…and *whatever-ally*. He had taken a step—a huge step—toward getting on with his life. What he had in mind for that life, she didn't know. And it didn't concern her.

She had issued an ultimatum. Kurt had chosen to protect his privacy over protecting their relationship. She no longer had to sit and stew over that man and his plans—or lack of them. They had cut those ties a few weeks ago, and it was time to make a new start. Him at Ezra's Holler. Her? Also at Ezra's Holler. It only made sense.

April had the capacity to grow, and God had just presented her with room to do it.

She could get over feeling sorry for herself and do some good for someone else, for Miss Cora. And if it gave her some insight into Kurt Muldoon and helped her forgive him so that she could move on… How could she *not* do it?

It sure beat sitting in a parking-lot median, playing in the dirt, singing, "Nobody likes me, everybody hates me…"

Guilt could not move her to action, but hope had. She put the trowel down, stood, swiped the dirt from her hands and asked with a smile, "Okay, Miss Cora. How soon can you be ready?"

Chapter Three

"I'm not a coward." Kurt lifted a large cardboard box from the bed of his pickup truck and twisted his head around to meet the unwavering gaze of his Australian shepherd, Matilda, sitting in the cab of the truck. "I'm not."

Matilda cocked her head, one ear raised.

"I know what you're thinking. That I'm running away from that alleged band of meddling matchmakers. But I was *going* to move out here sooner or later."

Matilda looked away.

Kurt hoisted the heavy box higher against his chest. "Okay, you got me there. Moonie Shelnutt's warning motivated me to make the move sooner rather than later. But that does not make it an act of cowardice."

The dog sneezed.

"Scoff all you want. But if the church ladies can't find me, they can't help me." Kurt rounded the bed of the truck and nodded toward the monstrosity of a house he planned to spend the rest of his life over-hauling—alone. "And that's just fine in my book. The last thing I need in my life right now is a romantic relationship—especially not a wife."

Matilda yawned.

"Yeah, yeah, you've heard it before, but it's true. I don't *need* anyone. Not to help me find a wife. Not to help me make this house into a home. Not for anything."

The dog watched Kurt walk past with what he could only describe as droll skepticism. He turned to face her.

"Marriage is not all companionship and romance, you know. It's a lot of hard work. More so if only one of you is doing the heavy lifting." His chest tightened like a fist, as if he could physically squeeze the life out of any emotions that might surface un-expectedly with his memories.

"You don't know what I went through at the hands of Wileyville's most well-meaning residents that first year after Carol died. The speculation. The unsolicited advice. The sickening overload of sympathy one minute, the snickering behind my back the next. And so much of it was my own fault."

The contents of the box shifted.

He staggered slightly, regained his footing and

dispensed with the swell of unwelcome sentiments in one harsh, exhaled breath.

"I won't go through that again—and I would never put anyone I cared about through it, either. You can count on that."

He knew the animal didn't understand a word he said. He was just projecting his own muddled feelings onto Matilda to better cope with them.

"Hey," he told the dog with her head cocked, "I'm a guy. That's what guys do."

And so long as he didn't have some woman standing by to point out his need for emotional maturity, he was going to go right on doing it, he thought as he headed for his empty house.

After a moment, Matilda leapt down from the seat and trotted up the walk ahead of him, brushing him with her tail as she did. He took that to mean that she didn't buy his brave words for one moment.

"Hey!" He hurried along behind the animal onto the wide steps of the airy, wooden front porch. "I will not accept that attitude from someone who gives her heart to anyone who will rub her belly and call her—"

Wham!

The screen door swung open so fast and so wide that it banged against the wall.

"Pretty girl," he concluded, clutching at the box to keep it from pitching forward.

"Uh. Oh, hi."

Never had three syllables carried so much impact for Kurt. Never had a pair of eyes elicited such sudden, unexpected emotion. An emotion he could not name.

Fear? No.

Regret? Perhaps. But not entirely.

Deliverance? There was that.

And more.

As to what and how much more, it was best not to dwell on that now, he decided.

"Hi," he managed to say, shifting the box in his arms as he added softly, "April."

April Shelnutt. Standing in *his* doorway, waiting for him to come home to *his* house. She looked… She looked as if she was where she always belonged.

Where he would always see her, even years from now, long after she had given up on him and shared a home with another man, a husband, and maybe children. He could hardly swallow just thinking of that day.

He must have been staring, hard.

April blinked, then tore her gaze away, glancing down. Her cheeks grew red and her shoulders rose and fell in sweet, shallow breaths.

And it hit him. If he kissed her now and asked her to forgive him for all the hurt he'd caused her or would ever cause her, she would do it.

Right here.

Right now.

No recriminations.

No regrets.

No reprisals.

So that was the last thing he could allow himself to do.

He stood frozen to the spot a moment before he got it together enough to ask "What are you doing here?"

She opened her mouth and glanced up. Her gaze met his. It seemed to say that he'd caught her off guard but had not taken her totally by surprise. "I, uh, I…"

She wet her lips. A totally innocent gesture that drove him half out of his mind. But not so much that he didn't recognize the struggle in her eyes. She had come here for a reason—more than one, probably— and right now, she was debating which, if any, she wanted to reveal to him.

Finally, she set her jaw and raised her head in something between a nod to direct his attention inside and a show of stubborn pride. "I brought Miss Cora out. She said you hadn't moved in yet."

"Oh." He nodded.

She tilted her head. A stray strand of hair fell across her neck, golden-brown against her pale skin.

It made him think of the way her hair fell in glossy waves when she didn't wear it in a braid, of how soft that hair felt between his work-roughened fingers. Suddenly, he wanted to touch her.

He thought of how good she smelled. He wanted to stand close to her and close his eyes.

He thought of how she'd made him laugh and

made him care. How she had trusted him and maybe, just maybe, loved him.

And he wanted to get as far away from her as possible.

"I thought I heard someone talking out here, so I came out to—" Her lashes fluttered.

"To what?" His heart beat faster. *To jump in my arms?* He knew better, but he wanted to hear it from her, wanted her to stand up to him, to show him he hadn't wounded her so much that she had lost the dignity and grace that had first drawn him to her.

Her hands flitted to her hair, her collar, to brush down the front of her khaki pants, then finally come to rest behind her back. Cool and businesslike, she took a deep breath and, without a trace of emotion, said, "I didn't think you'd be here."

"So you said." Her dignity and grace were intact. He smiled. He didn't mean to smile, but he couldn't help himself.

"I just wanted to make that clear."

"Got it."

"Okay, just so you know."

"I know."

"Now that that's out of the way." Her shoulders relaxed, a sly smile came over her face and she opened her arms. "I can't tell you how happy I am to see *you!*"

"Really?" He tried not to grin like a complete

fool. "After our last conversation, I didn't think you would ever speak to me again."

"I'm *not* speaking to you." Icicles could have formed on her words as she edged by him. "I'm talking to your dog. Hey, Matilda. How are you, girl?"

Matilda didn't merely wag her tail; her whole body shook with undisguised pleasure at the sight of April.

Kurt couldn't blame the old girl. If he had been a real dog instead of just acting like a hound toward this kind, caring woman, his tail would have given away his delight in seeing her again, as well.

A few slurps and giggles later, April stood and spun around to face him again. If seeing him here had thrown her, it didn't show. She appeared calm, rational and detached. "So what's with the box? Bringing a few things out at a time?"

"Moving in, actually."

"Moving in? Now? But Miss Cora said you planned to take your time."

He forced a shrug. "Plans change."

"So I've heard," she murmured.

But? She asked it with her eyes. With her stance. *How? When? Why?*

Kurt said nothing. Gave nothing away with his body language. If she wanted more of an explanation than that, she'd have to do what far too many of the good women of Wileyville did in those circumstances: make one up for herself. He had no intention of sharing his intentions with anyone. "Would you mind getting the door for me?"

"Sure." Quick on her feet, she raced up the steps, opened the screen door again and slipped inside the small foyer ahead of him. "Great house, by the way."

He nodded and stepped past her, careful not to so much as graze her arm with his. "Has good bones."

"It's in surprisingly fine shape." She let the door fall shut soundly. "I can see why you fell in love with it."

"Love?" He practically wrenched his neck as he turned to narrow his eyes on her and demand "Who said anything about love?"

"Well, not *you,* obviously. I just meant that I could see why you'd be drawn to it." She folded her arms over her soft jacket and tipped her head to one side. "It's so well-built. So quiet. So *isolated.*"

"Well, it would be," he muttered under his breath as he moved past her to place the box in the hallway, "if people didn't take it upon themselves to just up and come out here whenever they felt like it."

"I told you I brought Miss Cora out to gather some things." Her tone dripped with challenge, baiting him to suggest that she had come out here to spy on him or win him back. Try it, badge boy, her expression told him, and give me a reason to shoot a hole in that big, fat ego of yours. "Miss Cora said she had your permission, and I, for one, didn't have the heart to tell her that you have a history of changing your mind about things that matter most to other people."

He sighed and squinted down the long, dim hall toward the bright, open kitchen. If he made a run for it...

Kurt Muldoon, run from a woman? He gritted his teeth.

If he made a break, it wouldn't be April he would be running from; it would be himself. Because of the way April made him feel. As if he could actually outrun the ideas about hearth and home and happily ever after and other impossible fairy tales that her presence here put in his head.

He clenched his jaw to keep from blurting out anything foolish. Not that he was ever in any real danger of losing control.

He turned and found himself gazing directly into April's eyes.

Suddenly, the ten-room, two-story home felt as cramped as a closet, with only the two of them squeezed in toe-to-toe. He took in a breath and caught the scent of her skin lotion and knew he had to get out of there. "Where is dear old Miss Cora anyway?"

"Downstairs bedroom." April pointed in the general direction of the room at the south corner of the house. "She needed to lie down before we started back. Poor little thing. The trip just about wore her out, but then she insisted we walk through the garden."

"Garden?" The mention of it gave him the excuse to head for the porch again. Fresh air. That would do the trick. Clear his head. Give him room. "You can't mean that mass of weeds and tangled vines within those overgrown river-rock walls?"

"You know for a fact that's exactly what I mean." Her footsteps followed in hurried succession out onto the wide, shaded porch. "In fact, I'm supposed to be headed out there right now to get Miss Cora some shears from the shed."

He scratched his neck and frowned at the untended plot of land at the end of a curving stone walkway on the east side of the house. "I thought you said Miss Cora was resting."

"Miss Cora never rests. Not entirely. I did get her to lie down on the bed, though. Of course, that put her at the perfect angle to notice some snapped twigs on the dogwood outside her window, and she swore she couldn't get a moment's peace until I took care of them."

"Dogwood? There's a dogwood tree out here?"

She glared at him. "Dogwood, river birch, Japanese maple, not to mention all the more-common, local varieties. If you intend to take care of this place, you'd better acquaint yourself with it a whole lot better than you…"

He laughed. He sure did enjoy getting the fire up in that girl.

When she realized he'd goaded her on purpose,

her expression softened. "Sorry. The idea of these beautiful grounds going uncared for rattles my cage a bit. Promise me you'll take care of them?"

"Me? Promise? A man who has a history of changing my mind about things that matter most to other people?"

She did not apologize for her assessment. "Then hire someone to come out here and tend to the grounds at the very least."

"Hire someone? You mean hire you?"

"I don't need the work," she said softly. "Lots of people could do it."

"Yeah, but I don't want lots of people out here." And he meant that. "Besides, if I get the place looking too good, before I know, it I'll be roped into holding open houses and church youth-group bonfires and school tours."

"How horrible for you," she muttered. "You might actually have to act like a human being three or four times a year."

"Better get those shears before Miss Cora has a conniption."

"Hissy fit," she corrected, unsmiling.

"What?"

"Miss Cora is not self-righteous enough to have a conniption. She is, however, just spoiled enough, just proud enough and definitely aged-past-caring-what-people-think enough to pitch a first-class hissy fit."

"Conniption." He shook his head.

"Hissy fit," she countered, even as she started down the porch steps. "But to be on the safe side, I'd better see to that dogwood before—"

"April! April Shelnutt! What is keeping you, young lady? You think I have all the time in the world to wait for you while you do who knows what? Get back here!"

"You're right," he said softly. "Definitely a hissy fit."

"But not coming from the back bedroom." April turned her head.

Matilda barked at the sound that seemed to be coming from the far side of the house.

"I'm on my way, Miss Cora. Where are you?" April took off down the remaining porch steps, then ran toward the sound of Miss Cora's voice.

Matilda bounded after April, stopping on the walkway to turn and scold Kurt with a few sharp barks.

"I'm coming. I just…" He had made a decision not to chase after April romantically. That included throwing himself after her in some imagined crisis and letting himself get wrapped up in her pet projects. Besides, if he hoped to keep his thoughts from straying to how she looked with her braid swaying behind her or how she wore her heart on her sleeve over some silly situation or how easy it would be to run after her, catch her and take her in his arms and hear her say—

"Oh, Kurt! I need you and I need you *now!*"

Matilda barked again and tore off into the yard, rounding the big tree at the corner of the house just as April had done before her.

Kurt didn't bother with steps or sidewalks or trees. In a matter of seconds, he pounded down the length of the porch and leapt over the railing. He landed so hard that it jarred him to his back teeth. One, two, three strides and he all but stumbled over April, Miss Cora and the bare-limbed dogwood.

"I don't believe my eyes." Before he could stop it, one hard, heartfelt laugh burst through his clenched teeth.

Miss Cora raised her head and peered at him through the thin branches of the small tree. "I certainly would appreciate it if there was less laughing going on around here and a lot more rescuing of helpless little old ladies!"

He cleared his throat and moved to help April support the elderly woman, who was half in, half out of the first-floor window, hanging on to the dogwood for dear life.

"Miss Cora, what have you managed to do to yourself?"

"Me? I didn't do a thing. It's this house of yours, Sheriff. It's dangerous!"

"Only to people doing things that they were never meant to do. What is it you were trying to accomplish?"

"I got tired of waiting for that girl." She let loose

of the tree long enough to shake an accusatory finger at April. "She never came back with the shears, so I thought I'd just open up the window and break those twigs off myself."

April ducked under his arms. She made a slow assessment of the situation, brushing away bits of broken buds from Miss Cora's arm to make sure she hadn't been injured. "So you stuck half your body out the window to wrestle with a dogwood?"

Kurt met his onetime Sunday school teacher's eyes. "Looks like the dogwood won."

"It's not the dogwood. It's this window that's fell shut on my sit-down! That's what's got me in a fix."

"Window fell shut on your sit-down?" Kurt repeated slowly.

"That's what she said." April placed her hand on his back. "And if you don't want that scrappy sprite of a ninety-year-old to take a switch to *your* sit-down, you better get her out of this."

"Me?"

"Sure, you. Big he-man sheriff. I thought you did everything by yourself. Other people only complicate things for you, and the last thing *I'd* want to do is complicate—"

"I got it." He held his hand up. He made a quick once-over of Miss Cora's predicament. Anyone else he would have pulled out or pushed back in or even left awhile to contemplate the recklessness of her actions.

Matilda paced and whined.

Miss Cora tipped her nose up and sniffed, a predictable way of warning that she was not at all pleased with his dawdling.

April set her lips in a thin line and folded her arms, her shoulders underneath Miss Cora's upper body for support.

He knew what April wanted.

And he knew what *he* wanted. He wanted April gone from his home before he had a chance to think about how right it felt to have her here. And before anyone in Wileyville got wind of her visit and the buzz about them started.

To do that, he had to extricate Miss Cora from his dogwood tree without hurting or humiliating her. If Miss Cora showed up in town with so much as a scrape or spreading the story of how the sheriff had done her wrong, all his hopes of hiding out here and keeping his ownership of the place a secret would evaporate.

"Go into the house," he told April, his jaw so tight he didn't know how he formed the words. "We'll work together."

April smiled and it was a little bit smirky, too. Then she patted Miss Cora and shifted the woman's weathered hand onto Kurt's arm. "If you'll excuse me, ma'am, I believe our sheriff needs me."

"I didn't say that," he barked.

"You wouldn't, though, would you?" she asked,

sliding out from under the woman in the tree and leaving her in Kurt's care.

The iciness of April's gaze took him by surprise. Though he had no right to expect anything more than coolness from her ever again, he couldn't help feeling sad. Not for his loss but for hers. What happened between them had changed this warm, vibrant woman, like a late frost changes the blossoms and fruit of a budding garden. *He* had done this to her. And all he could say was, "I won't say something just because you want to hear it, April. That's not fair to either one of us. But I would *appreciate* your help in this. And then I'd *appreciate* your leaving my house and not coming back again."

Chapter Four

"He'd *appreciate* my leaving and not coming back? Does he really think I am such a ninny that I don't know what he's really saying?"

April talked to animals. She talked to plants. And as a woman who had lived all of her adult life alone, she talked to herself more than she liked to admit. She took some comfort in the fact that, so far, she had not taken to answering herself.

Until now.

"Yes, that's exactly what he thinks. That he can alter a single word and I will be too…what? Dopey? Naive? Too enamored by his macho posturing to decipher the riddle that is Kurt Muldoon? *Appreciate* my leaving and not coming back?"

She rounded the corner of the house and moved from the shade into the light. The fading afternoon sun stung her eyes. She frowned and squinted, picking up her pace even as her ire rose.

"I know what he meant. He *needs* for me to leave and not come back. *Needs.* But will he ever admit that? Not likely. Not any more than I could ever look him in the eye and admit…"

Thud, thud, thud.

April couldn't distinguish the hammering of her heart from the pounding of her feet over the uneven ground. Nor could she reconcile her feelings for Kurt with her need to purge herself of the man once and for all.

I came here to find a way to forgive him. Maybe this is the way. Maybe by working with him to help Miss Cora, I will see the good in him again and then…

"Then what?" she grumbled, even as she headed for the porch steps.

Then I will drive off, leaving him here to watch me go. Me finally taking action. Not just shielding myself and hoping to withstand what is thrown my way.

"I'm moving on. Leaving Kurt behind. Not just symbolically but in truth. In power. In a car that can kick dust up on his boots as I go," she whispered, hoping that saying the words aloud would give them weight and significance.

It didn't.

Truth? Power? Dust?

"Ugh," she groaned. "I am such a sap."

She hit the steps, then the screen door. It squeaked open, then slammed shut behind her.

Face it, she had come here on a shaky pretense at best, and now the smartest thing she could do for herself—and Kurt, for that matter—was to rescue Miss Cora, hightail it back to town and never look back.

That would have been a whole lot easier if she didn't know that, if she did happen to look back, Kurt would be *here,* living his very own personal brand of happily ever after. Alone.

"Hold still, Miss Cora. All that wiggling is loosening the paint on the window sash and making it stick to the frame. You're going to get yourself wedged in permanently."

Okay, so maybe he wouldn't get that happily-ever-after-alone deal. Maybe he would have to share his mellow years with the old lady stuck in his window. It would serve him right, of course. But Miss Cora deserved better.

"I'm here, Miss Cora. I'm in the room, Kurt. What now?" She reached out to put a steadying hand on the small elderly woman's, uh, shoes?

Really, where else could she grab hold of the old gal without offending Miss Cora's, um, sense of decorum?

"Put your arms around her on that end," Kurt ordered.

"*End* being the operative word," April muttered.

"And when you've latched onto her, I'll shove the

window up. She's jammed herself in pretty tight, so brace yourself for her to come tumbling backward."

"Latched onto...shove...tumbling backward." With every word, her sticklike legs flailed in the air, sending multiple lace-trimmed layers of half slips shimmying lower and lower. "You two take extra care with me. I am a *lady,* after all."

"I'm trying to remember that, Miss Cora." April chewed her lip as she studied the situation, then did the only thing she thought Miss Cora would put up with without trying to do April any bodily harm. She seized her thick-stockinged ankles.

Miss Cora kicked like a mule at the first touch.

"April? You okay?" Kurt called through the opening. "How's it look from your side of the window?"

Frilly, she wanted to report, glancing at the slipping slips, but then her eyes fell on the thrashing nurses' shoes and the scuff mark they'd left on her inner arm. "It looks dangerous. You?"

"Might look the same if Miss Cora follows up on her threat to take a bite out of my arm if I'm not careful. But I don't think she's going to try it."

"Because you're so handsome and charming?" April drawled.

"No. Because I'm so thick-skinned and tough."

April couldn't argue with that.

Through the window, she could see him crouching low to put himself eye-to-eye with his tiny, white-haired nemesis as he said, "And if she sinks her dentures into my arm, it wouldn't hurt me one bit."

"I don't have in my dentures, young man," she said, followed by a kick, wiggle and great show of gnashing of gums by the old gal. "But if I took a notion, I could still chomp down on you something fierce."

"She's not lying." April bent low, too, to make sure that her voice carried through the opening. "I've seen her crack walnuts with those gums, Kurt."

"Then maybe she should have *bit* the twigs off and saved you and me all this commotion."

"Bit the twigs? Now there's a picture. Me in a tree, gnawing off branches." Miss Cora cackled and, in doing so, relaxed just enough to allow April a shot at moving in close to wrap her arms around her frail hips and hang on for dear life.

"I've got her."

"I've got the window. Hang on."

He placed his hands under the window sash and strained to raise it.

The wooden frame groaned but did not budge.

April anchored her feet wider.

Kurt tried again, his face growing beet red.

"You all right, Sheriff?" Miss Cora asked. "You look sort of like Daddy did just before he joined the heavenly choir."

April jerked her head up.

Oh, no. Kurt Muldoon was not going to have a

heart attack helping April help someone who was helping herself in a rummage of his yet-to-be-lived-in house. If that happened and he lived, he'd never forgive her. Which would totally negate her ever being able to forgive him. Talk about your quagmire in the road to moving on with your life!

And if he died...

"Deep, steady breaths," April told him, trying to keep the panic out of her voice. Kurt could not die. Not this way. Not with his last images of her as angry and with her face pressed up against Miss Cora's behind! "We can do this."

"We? *We?*" He repositioned his hands, his body still beneath the elderly woman to keep her propped comfortably in place. "In case you haven't noticed, I'm the one doing all the physical work here."

"And Miss Cora and I both appreciate it," she said, realizing too late that he might take that as sarcasm.

He grunted.

"Just one more good, clean push," she urged.

If the police scanner in Kurt's truck could have picked this up, the listeners might have thought they were eavesdropping on a total role-reversal birthing of a baby. Which was why it amused April to no end when the window popped open and she tugged Miss Cora gently inside, steadied the old gal on her feet and peered out to call to Kurt "It's a girl!"

Kurt didn't so much as crack a smile. He did tear

his pants, though, as he came crawling through the window a few moments after Miss Cora had cleared the way.

He stopped to, well, she wasn't sure what he was doing—poking his finger in the ragged little rip at the knee—other than making the tear worse. If ever a man needed a woman to help him deal with life's little difficulties....

He glanced up and met her gaze with an accusatory glare.

April swallowed hard, glad they couldn't hear his inner monologue. If they could, Miss Cora might demand they wash his mouth out with soap. And April just did not want to be that close to him right now.

Okay, not strictly true. She wouldn't have minded giving him a hug. Just to thank him for what he'd done for Miss Cora. And maybe tossing in how very relieved she was that he hadn't dropped dead of a heart attack before she could make peace with him. But he wouldn't have *appreciated* her telling him those things any more than he'd *appreciate* her hugging him while he was all out of breath and sweaty and adorable in that grumpy, rumpled way of his.

"Why did I do this?" He rubbed his hand over his forehead.

"It was the Christian thing to do, Sheriff, to give aid to someone who couldn't care for herself." Miss Cora placed her hand gingerly over the place on her body where the window had delivered its stiffest insult.

Kurt smiled. "No, not why did I help you. Why did I climb in the window afterward?"

"Oh, that? That was the *manly* thing to do." The old gal's eyes twinkled. "To show off for someone who couldn't care less what you do."

Kurt blushed. At least, April thought he blushed. Maybe it was anger flooding his cheeks or the remnants of his recent exertion.

"I have to go let Matilda in," he muttered, making a quick exit.

"My goodness, that man sure is darling." Miss Cora limped a step or two, then lowered herself to perch on the edge of the chair she had pushed to the windowsill to help her climb out. "You ever consider setting your cap for him, girl?"

"Setting my cap?"

"You know." She churned her skinny little arms in the air to simulate running. "Letting him chase you until you catch him?"

"Afraid that's a bit of a lost cause, Miss Cora. He doesn't want to chase me, and *I* certainly don't want to catch him."

"You sure? You two look powerfully cute together."

Powerfully cute. The perfect reason to reorder your whole life around the hope of somehow, someday, establishing a relationship. Maybe she and

Miss Cora were more alike than April wanted to admit. Because the notion did hold some appeal.

She looked toward the hallway beyond the bedroom door and heard the screen door swing open with a screech. Kurt whistled for his dog. The scurrying of paws on the porch was followed by Matilda's master greeting her with more open praise and affection than he had ever dared to show April.

She sighed. "I might as well set my cap for the man in the moon, Miss Cora. I'd stand a better chance of finding happily ever after."

"Don't give up hope, dear. There's always hope."

"Of course there is, but hope without some good sense is a sad, sad thing. It's like planting kumquats and expecting tomatoes just because you really want tomatoes."

"Tomatoes?" The white head lifted. "Whatever happened to those prizewinning tomatoes that I—"

April took the old woman by the elbow and eased her up from the chair. "Here, Miss Cora, let's get you to the bed."

"Don't do that!" Kurt stood in the doorway and thrust out his hand.

"Why not?" April asked, trying not to notice the way his sudden jerky movement made his hair fall across his forehead.

"If you lay her on the bed, she might fall asleep."

Matilda sat behind him, her cocked head following April and Kurt as each spoke.

"What if she does fall asleep?" April asked.

Kurt frowned. "What if she, uh, has a concussion?"

"A concussion?" April guided the woman to the bedside. "From having a window sash pinch her on the backside?"

Miss Cora cackled, weakly.

The bedsprings creaked, not so weakly.

The mattress compressed under the slight weight of her old body.

As April reached for the white antique duvet, she muttered, "If I ever need first aid, remind me not to call the Wileyville sheriff's department, Miss Cora. I might end up with a tourniquet around my neck for a stubbed toe."

Another feeble laugh from the old gal.

April unfolded the duvet and marveled at the delicate fields of lavender and yellow flowers flawlessly embroidered around the edges and in the corners. And not a bit of dust or even a musty odor rose from the fabric. She gave it a shake to fluff it a bit, then…

Kurt's hand came down on hers, gentle but firm.

April's gaze fell first to where they touched, then slowly, she raised her head to face him. It had been a long time since they stood this close. A long time since his hand held hers. A long time since she dared to meet his gaze full on for fear of what emotion she would see in his eyes. Or what she would *not* see.

"Take her into the kitchen." If he felt anything at

all right now, he hid it well. Or maybe she just couldn't read him anymore.

April tugged her hand free and stepped away from him. "Why?"

"The, uh, the light is better in there." He rubbed his thumb into the palm of the hand that had held her moments before. "And, uh, if she got hurt, you know, if she has any bruises or cuts, we can see them better in there."

He had a point. They should check out Miss Cora. April stepped back. "But if we take her anyplace for that, it should be the bathroom."

Kurt took a side step directly into her path. "We can, uh, also get her a drink of water in the kitchen."

"What?" April tossed the duvet across the foot of the bed. It missed Miss Cora's feet entirely and slid off into a pile on the floor. April sighed, bending down as she asked, "You don't have water in the bathroom?"

"Yeah, there's water, but I don't have a glass in there."

"Then go get one from the kitchen." She snatched up one corner of the duvet, then gathered it into her arms. "Miss Cora and I will head to the bathroom."

"But the kitchen is closer to—"

April straightened and nearly bonked her head on Kurt's chin.

"The door," he finished softly, his face just inches from hers. The floorboards creaked under the shifting weight of his boots.

"The door?" What was that emotion she saw in his eyes? Regret? Hope? Hunger? She wet her lips. Her skin drew up into goose bumps. She bunched up the duvet between them. "Which we need for...?"

"Leaving," he said.

"Leaving?" She blinked.

"As in exiting. Hitting the trail. Beating a hasty retreat."

Not regret, hope or hunger.

"Retreat." She laid the duvet over the footboard of the old bed and shook her head. "That's your solution for everything, isn't it?"

"No."

She glanced at him.

He held his ground. He did not budge. But he did clear his throat and look away. "Let's just get her into the kitchen and then we can argue all we want about where to put her."

Gnarrrrrp.

Kurt and April turned their heads to find Miss Cora curled up on the bed on her side, snoring her primped and permed and peppered-with-sticks-and-leaves head off.

April nabbed the duvet and began to unfurl it over her small body. "Guess that settles the where-to-put-her debate for now."

"You could wake her," Kurt whispered.

"You want her awake, *you* wake her." She tucked

the soft fabric in place. "Isn't that your way? Do everything for yourself? Don't ever rely on anyone?"

"I rely on other people all the time, April."

"Rely on them—?" she glanced down to make sure Miss Cora looked comfy, then pivoted to confront Kurt "—or use them?"

His green eyes flashed. His mouth twitched. His gaze dipped, the only acknowledgment that he understood why she said what she said, and he exhaled long and low. "I'm sorry if you feel that I did, but I never used you, April."

"Yeah, right, and you never *appreciated* me, either." She pushed past him, reached the door and stepped right on Matilda's outstretched paw.

Yikes!

April gasped. "I am so sorry, girl. Are you all right?"

In one step, Kurt was behind her, his chest pressed to her back, his hand around her upper arm to steady her on her feet. "Are *you* all right?" he asked.

"I'm fine," she said. "Let me go."

"Go where?"

She looked down the hallway to where the sun streamed in the open front door. Then she looked toward the other end and the dim kitchen. At last, she looked down at the dog she had just unintentionally hurt.

Matilda lifted her head and watched April with the most kind, forgiving eyes that served to remind her that she had come to Ezra's Holler for a reason.

"Or, more importantly," Kurt pressed on, "why are you here? Why are you *really* here?"

Moment of truth.

I came here to make peace with our relationship—or our lack of one.

Or moment of indecision?

Not that it's any of your business, having excused yourself from any connection to me whatsoever.

Could they be one and the same moment?

April couldn't help it. When he asked her in such a general way like that, how could she but wonder if she owed him anything but a general answer? She wouldn't lie. But she found herself hard-pressed to spill her every thought and intimate motivation to a man who found it impossible to even share a meal in public with her.

"I told you before, we came out here so Miss Cora could check for some personal items."

"And when you told me that, I remember thinking that it might not be the whole answer."

Note to self: never again date someone trained in observation and deduction.

"You told me why *Miss Cora* came out here today." His grip on her loosened, but only a little. His breath felt warm on her neck as he refused to let her off the hook. "Now tell me why *you* did."

"Because…" She shut her eyes and tried not to think too much about him standing so close. She straightened her spine and put a little steel in her tone. "How else would Miss Cora get out here? Hitchhike?"

"Now you've gone from giving me partial answers to giving me no answers at all."

She looked at him over her shoulder. "Why do you need an answer from me at all?"

He clenched his jaw. "I'd like one."

"But you don't need one." She huffed and nodded, wondering if he knew that she was only stalling while she tried to decide how much, if anything, to tell him about her quest in coming here.

"What did you hope to gain by coming out here, April?"

"*Gain?* You make me sound like some plotting… Oh!" She was overreacting, but he'd embarrassed her with the implication, which just served to remind her how foolish he made her feel when he'd rejected her for simply wanting to be seen in public with him. As if on some silly emotional seesaw, the two insults bounced up and down and back and forth in her brain, gaining momentum until what had once been only pent-up energy unleashed itself on him. She spun around and stepped into the hallway, minding Matilda as she dragged him by the front of his plaid shirt.

"You have the nerve to get on your high horse and talk down to me about coming out here to gain something after the way you treated me!"

"April, I didn't—"

"After you demanded that I engage in sneaking

around, keeping our relationship a secret even from my own family? That we never so much as acknowledge each other in public?"

"We've been through all this, April, and I had my—"

"And the moment I said I could no longer sneak and weasel and practically lie about my feelings for you, you drop me?"

"If you would just let me get a word—"

"And now you have the gall to suggest I came slinking out here under the guise of helping a sweet, little old lady in order to—to what?" She flung open her arms and groaned, then took a few steps toward the kitchen before turning to find him on her heels. "Spy on you?"

"No, I never said—"

"Get my hooks back into you?" She folded her arms and tapped her boot on the floor.

"I, uh, you see, when I came out here and found you—"

"Don't even." She threw her hand up to keep him from finishing that thought because she'd heard his explanations before and they never made her feel any better about him or herself. "The point is, I didn't come out here to do any of that."

She headed for the kitchen again, full steam ahead.

He followed, never more than a couple of steps behind. "Why did you come out here then?"

He was never going to let this go. Not until she told him the truth. She spun around, fired up and ready to confront him. "I came out here to try to find a way to forgive you so that I could be done with you once and for all."

He halted dead in his tracks. Paused. Took it in. Then smiled, slowly. "How's it working so far?"

She exhaled, and with her breath went a bit of the indignation. "Not so good."

His smile broadened.

"Don't laugh at me." Her stomach clenched. "Don't you dare laugh at me."

"I'm not laughing, honestly. I just—" he held his hands up, the sign of surrender "—I just realized how much I've missed you."

She blinked. "Really?"

"Actually, no."

"Oh."

"I realized *that* about ten minutes after we broke up."

"Broke up?" She mustered something like a chuckle at that and leaned her back against the wall. It was less a sign of surrender and more a sign of ceasefire for the time being. "Wouldn't we have to actually have been a couple to break up?"

He braced his arm against the opposite wall and casually kicked one ankle over the other, lulled into enough of a sense of appeasement to joke. "If we were never a couple and never broke up, then why did you have to come out to my new place to try to get over me?"

Only April didn't find his joke all that amusing. "Get *over* you?"

He straightened.

She did the same. "I think what's called for here is for you to get over yourself!"

"What? I only meant that—"

"I came out here to find a way to *forgive* you, Muldoon." She made quotation marks in the air with her fingers to emphasize the word *forgive,* hoping the action might penetrate his thick layer of ego. "Because, unlike some people, I am self-aware enough to know that you have to resolve things within yourself. You can't just push all your problems onto other people and pretend they are the root of your issues."

He raised an eyebrow at her claim. "I thought you came out here for Miss Cora."

"Her, too. Really, it's not like she could ever come out here on her own."

"I would have brought her."

"Oh, please."

"What?"

"You?"

"What's wrong with me?"

"I hope to be home before dark, so let's not even start on *that* topic." She made her way into the kitchen and began rooting around the cupboards for a glass to get Miss Cora some water when she woke up. "But we can address why it's totally ridiculous to think you could handle Miss Cora on your own."

He crossed the threshold, pivoted an old, painted wooden chair around on one leg and plunked himself down, his arms folded over the back. "I'm listening."

"She's old, Kurt. She forgets things. Forgets what she wants and who she's talking to."

"I never think of her as feeble."

"That's just it. She's *not* feeble, as you might have noticed with the whole climbing-out-into-a-tree episode. Her wiry little body can get up to all manner of things that someone thinking straight would know better than to ever try."

"Maybe you should have told her that there'd be no point to coming out here when I could bring any personal things I found to her."

She scowled at him. "That's just mean."

"Is it?" He frowned. "I didn't intend for it to be mean. I just thought it would save everyone a lot of trouble."

"Save *you* a lot of trouble."

"And you. And, as it turns out, Miss Cora and her sit-down."

"Not everybody conducts their lives with their eyes on what will save them the most trouble," she said, finally finding the glasses and taking one down.

"If that's meant to be a characterization of me, it's an unfair one. People make trouble for me all day long. It's the nature of my job, the nature of my family, and if I let it, it would become the nature of my very existence."

His very existence? April weighed the claim as she turned on the tap, waiting for the water to run clear before rinsing out the jelly-jar glass she had found. On the one hand, Kurt's claim sounded cornier than a whole pot of hominy poured over a skillet full of cornbread, as Miss Cora might have put it. On the other hand, he made a point about his job and his family throwing trouble his way at every opportunity. Unspoken, of course, was being a hometown boy who came back to Wileyville with far too much personal baggage and way too little wife and family in tow to suit the locals—another point in his favor.

And it irked April to no end.

"I came out here to close the door on whatever it was between us. That's it, that's all." She straightened, water glass in hand, imagining her shoulders reaching from one side of the narrow kitchen to the other and her unflappable voice reaching to the heights of the twelve-foot ceiling. "I did not come out here to moon over what might have been. I came out here to close the door on you, badge boy, and, mark my words, that door will be swinging shut as soon as that sweet, little old lady wakes up."

"Where's that girl that never brought me my tomatoes?" The craggy voice sounded more distant than it should have, muffled even, but that did not take the tartness from its demand. "Somebody tell her to get in here before I take after her with a switch."

Kurt tipped his head toward the hallway behind him. "Guess you two will be leaving soon then."

"Coming, Miss Cora." She brushed by him. "Yes, we will be going soon but not soon enough to suit me."

One step. Two. And then...

She stared at the hallway floor, littered with Miss Cora's clothes leading right up to the bathroom door.

"Or not. I hope you give us enough time to get Miss Cora dressed before you toss us out!" April went to the door and knocked. "Hello? You all right in there?"

The door crept open just enough for the woman inside to peer out with one eye. "There you are. I called and called for you."

"I'm here now. Is there a problem?"

"Problem?" The one eye batted, her voice dripping honey. "What makes you think that?"

"Uh, because you're holed up in a bathroom in someone else's home stripped down to your un—"

"Hush, girl!" She placed a gnarled finger to her pale lips. "Don't look now, but there's a man standing behind you."

"Unmentionables," April finished.

Kurt made a sound. A chuckle maybe. Or a

harrumph. It didn't matter. April kept her attention fixed on the crack in the doorway and the necessity of coaxing Miss Cora back into her clothes and out of the house.

"I brought you a glass of water." She made the offering, thinking it might make the old gal open the door.

Miss Cora slipped her hand out and snatched the glass, spilling droplets of cold water onto April's wrist, pants and boots.

"Why don't you let me inside there to help you?" April asked, extending her arm behind her in hopes that Kurt would know what to do as she added "I'll bring in your dress and we'll—"

"I'm not getting back into that dress. Bring me my nightclothes."

"You didn't let her bring nightclothes out here, did you?"

April swung her elbow back to signal him to be quiet and missed the man by a mile. "We didn't bring any nightclothes, Miss Cora. If you recall, we only came out here to gather a few things, then head straight back to Wileyville. You didn't say anything about planning to spend the night."

"I *didn't* plan to spend the night," the plaintive voice whined. "But then I didn't plan for Lollie's boy to let the window squash my dignity, either."

"Hey!" Kurt edged forward, ready to protect his good name.

A gut reaction. April knew he couldn't help himself. After all, a sheriff who earned himself a reputation for squashing little old ladies? That would give people *plenty* to talk about!

"Cool it," April told him. "Let me get to the bottom of this, will you?"

"You, too." Miss Cora sniffed. "Making a joke at your old Sunday school teacher's expense."

"Miss Cora, I didn't mean—"

"It's too much, I tell you. It's why I will not go back to the home with a bruised backside. Can you imagine the kind of fun people would have with that? How much they will all want to stick their noses in my business? No, Missy, I am not going back until I can face them folks the way a good lifelong Christian lady should—sitting down."

Chapter Five

"You know what we have to do, don't you, Kurt?"

Rush the bathroom door and wrestle Miss Cora back into her clothes? Carry her piggyback all the way to Wileyville? Back the truck up to the porch, throw the duvet from the bedroom over her head and then scoot her out the door and into the truck bed before she knew what hit her? He was game for anything—anything short of bringing other people out to his new house and into his soon-to-be new life.

"We have to call a doctor."

He took a deep breath and let it out slowly. "I know."

"I can't believe it wasn't our first response. We should have dialed 911 right away."

"911? For getting stuck in a window?" He rubbed his forehead and shut his eyes to keep himself from launching into a lecture about the misuses of 911 emergency services. Or pointing out that the call from her cellphone would have been routed to the sheriff's department and picked up by the radio in his truck, the decision to send help or not based on *his* determination. "She needs to be checked out, but it's the kind of thing we can arrange ourselves. We don't need to go through the emergency system."

He had her.

One thing he learned from the short time they had spent together: April Shelnutt hated being "had." She liked taking control of any given situation, even if she had to stoop to goading a county sheriff to do so.

"You're the one who thought she might have a concussion."

He chuckled, just enough to show that she'd made her point, then added, "I didn't really think that."

"I know." She smiled. Her gaze dipped downward.

He took a deep breath to keep from reaching out to lift her chin and make her face him.

She sighed and looked toward the bathroom where Miss Cora had locked herself. "You just wanted us out of your house. And now look what's happened."

"Careful, tomato girl," he said all reserved when really he wanted to just put his arm around her and kiss her hair, her cheek, her petal-soft lips. Instead, he took a step back and leaned against the wall, his gaze never leaving her face. "You almost sounded sympathetic toward me for a minute there."

"Did I?" She shook her head. "Maybe you should call 911 then. Get them to send someone out to haul me away before I lose all my animosity toward you and start thinking it might not be such a bad thing to stay out here and tend to Miss Cora."

"Animosity? Is that really what it's got to between us?"

She didn't answer. And that was the only answer he needed. The only answer his long-ago battered heart could have taken.

"So it's agreed then? We call an ambulance? Paramedics from the fire department?"

He held his hand up. "Let's try something else first."

He rapped his knuckles softly on the bathroom door.

"Yes?" Miss Cora singsonged sweetly as if she was sitting at a lace-covered table inside, waiting for her maid to bring her afternoon tea.

"Miss Cora?" He cleared his throat, trying to keep his tone cordial but firm. "Miss Cora, do you know the name of your personal physician?"

"What kind of silly question is that? One of those ridiculous memory tests they keep sending social workers around to ask me?"

"No." He glanced at April.

She shook her head in a way that said let

someone who knows what she's dealing with
handle this. "Miss Cora? You know you can't stay
here overnight unless your doctor clears it with the
staff at Evergreen Meadows."

"Then call my doctor and see to getting that
done." The queen had spoken.

Kurt dipped his head in a show of respect. "To do
that, I'll have to know your doctor's name."

"My doctor told me not to tell that information to
just anybody."

"She doesn't know it." Kurt pinched the bridge of
his nose and began plotting how to keep his name and
April's from getting linked and how to keep his name
from being mentioned in the story the EMTs would
certainly relate when they later told the colorful tale of
the white-haired lady with the black-and-blue
backside.

"Bring the phone in here and I'll call Dr. Joyce
my own self," Miss Cora offered.

"Dr. Joyce? Your doctor is Dr. Joyce?"

"How'd you know that?" Shock and accusation
tinged the old woman's tone.

Kurt shut his eyes and shook his head.

April swatted his arm. "If Miss Cora catches you
laughing at her, she won't be the only one in the
house who will need medical attention."

"Yes, ma'am." He fixed his face in an expression that would have made his old army drill
sergeant proud. "Only I hope you don't expect Dr.

Joyce to be dispensing that medical attention on either of us."

"Why not?"

"She hasn't seen patients in years."

"She hasn't? You sure?"

"Absolutely." He had not one shred of doubt. "She was my mother's doctor, and when Mom told me she couldn't go to her anymore and didn't know what to do about it, that's when I made up my mind that I had to move back to Wileyville after I left the Army. You know, that moment of realization everybody has—that your parents aren't young anymore. That there isn't anyone to look after them unless you do."

"Unless one of your parents is Moonie Shelnutt and everybody looks out for him all the time."

He considered telling her that having a parent a whole lot of people love wasn't what he'd consider an insurmountable problem. But to say something like that revealed a lot more about the speaker than the people being spoken to or about. So he kept the thought to himself and feigned a sudden interest in the yellowing wallpaper in the long, narrow hallway. "Anyway, that's why I know Dr. Joyce can't be Miss Cora's doctor."

"Where's that phone?" the old woman demanded, rattling the doorknob but not unlocking the door. "I know where to get the number if that's the holdup. I have it written in the blue address book in my handbag. You have my permission to look it up and dial before you hand the phone over to me. But hop to it."

"You heard the lady. Start hopping." He swept his hand out. "Fast like a bunny."

April shot him a look that said she'd rather turn him into rabbit stew.

Not that he cared if he got in a little hot water. He was a hard-nosed army man after all. A sheriff. A loner. A…man.

He didn't need anyone's approval. Least of all, April Shelnutt's. He wrapped his arms across his chest and stood with his feet wide on the old hardwood floor.

She gave him one last look—softer this time, and not without nuance. She didn't have to say another word. He got the message. Got it? He was probably broadcasting it loud and clear with his own expression. *I wish things were different.*

But things were what they were. The product of a past that neither of them could alter. He broke eye contact, squinting toward the fading afternoon sun spilling in through the old screen door.

April moved past him. "I'm going to call that doctor and get this all cleared up."

"Call whoever you want." He watched her, trying not to let the sway of her braid, the determined thrum of her boot steps, the way the sunlight created a halo around her retreating figure burn themselves into his memory. Living here alone, without her, would be hard enough without those memories seared in his mind. "It won't change anything. Dr. Joyce isn't practicing anymore, and that means Miss Cora either isn't competent or isn't cooperating."

Kurt's declaration was still hanging in the air when Dr. Joyce finished her examination, then turned and smiled at them in that way of benevolent country doctors who enjoy dosing local authority figures with humble pie.

"I'm so glad you went ahead and called me, despite the wild notion *somebody* had that I had stopped practicing. Miss Cora will be fine in a day or so."

"A day or *so?*"

"Yes, a day or so." She shook her hands to dry them in the basin, then came to stand in the doorway. Between the shadows lingering in the hallway and the low-watt bulb in the bathroom, it was hard to guess the doctor's age. Her dark hair had silver sprigs here and there, but her rounded cheeks had no lines and still shone with rosy good humor. "Two, maybe four days—you know, whatever it takes."

"Four?" Kurt scratched his head.

"No more than six." Dr. Joyce gave him a hearty pat on the back.

"No more than—"

"Stop talking now." April seized him by the elbow and leaned in to whisper "Have you noticed that every time you open your mouth, Miss Cora ends up staying another few days?"

"Not to worry. Like I told you when you called, I live less than a mile away. I'll stop in once a day to check on her." The robust lady doc spoke directly to April.

Made sense, he supposed. April had not mentioned his buying the house to the woman, and he certainly hadn't felt inclined to volunteer the information.

So the doctor seemed to assume that, since April had brought Miss Cora out to Ezra's Holler, she would be the one taking responsibility for her.

"I guess you'll do the same, Sheriff?"

"I, uh…" He glanced at April.

April inched backward from him and folded her hands in front of her, all formal and distant as if she was addressing a passing acquaintance. "I don't think that will be necessary, Sheriff."

"Too bad." Dr. Joyce gave Kurt the once-over. Not a doctor-sizing-someone-up-for-potential-health-problems once-over, either. The kind of head-to-toe, frank-and-friendly going-over an interested party with no time for romantic games gave the opposite sex.

Kurt had seen that look before from women his age—well, from women of every age. When you lived in a town with so few male prospects and you were a guy with the goods—the goods Wileyvillestyle, meaning a man with standing in the community, sitting comfortably financially and not generally known for lying like a dog—you got used to women not wasting any time letting you know that they found you attractive.

Except April.

She had never fawned over him or flirted outrageously with him. She had never done crazy things to get his attention or enlisted the aid of her friends and family to set them up, as so many other women had. Whether April had known it or not, her seeming lack of interest had drawn him to her even more. A woman who respected herself and him and the privacy of their relationship—he couldn't imagine being with anyone who didn't possess those qualities.

The doctor gave his upper arm a squeeze. "With you stopping in over here, I'd have looked forward to running into you every day."

"Guess you'll just have to settle for me and your patient," April said, looking peeved at the good doctor's attention toward him.

Before he could play the potential rivalry up big—if he had been so inclined—Dr. Joyce was leaning into the room where Miss Cora lay resting.

"My *favorite* patient," she said, pulling the door shut to give the old gal some quiet. Then she turned, stepped over Matilda, gave April and Kurt a nod that said "Come with me and we'll talk" and headed for the front door. "She was my very first patient, you know. Lots of people around here didn't want a female doctor. Even though it was the 1980s in the rest of the world, in Wileyville, some were barely out of the Depression in their mind-set. But Miss Cora marched herself into my office and then made it known that I was all right. After that, things just grew, one patient at a time. Oh, look who I'm telling. You both know how things are here. Slow on the uptake, but once they take hold, the roots run deep."

Kurt moved ahead of the women to hold open the door for them. In some ways, he still carried those old traditions from Wileyville with him and always would.

"Guess you know about those roots, Sheriff." Dr. Joyce stepped out onto the porch, then twisted her head to ask. "Brought you back after how many years away?"

"Too many," he muttered when what he really meant was "not enough." "Of course, I didn't come back because of my ties to the town. I came back because…" With all three of them now outside, he let the door fall shut with a whop.

"Dr. Joyce, why did you tell my mother you weren't seeing patients anymore?"

"I didn't."

"But she said—"

"I told your mother I wouldn't see *her* anymore. Not as long as she insisted on prying into the personal business of people in my waiting room and then rushing off to Owtt's Eatery or the beauty shop or church and telling everybody who she saw there and what she thought they had. I didn't want to do it, to cut her off. I gave her every opportunity to change, but she didn't, and that's really all I can say on the matter."

"All you can say? Wish my mother felt the same way." He nodded. "I don't know why she does that."

"Maybe she's lonely," April said softly.

"Lonely? *My* mother? When does she have time to be lonely? She's always busy running from one social group to another, from one volunteer job to checking in on things at the family furniture store."

April went to the porch rail and raised her face toward the setting sun. Her face glowed golden and her golden-brown hair appeared dark in the shadows created by the roof. "Sometimes people try to lose themselves in the crowd to try to convince themselves that they aren't as lost as they feel."

Was that some kind of personal confession? Had April needed to take their relationship out into the open to make herself believe it was real? Had he cheated her out of that? Unlike his mama, she wasn't going to tell him outright.

"Or maybe your mother talks all the time about anything and anyone because she's afraid," Dr. Joyce suggested.

"Of what? A few seconds of silence?" He chuckled.

April and the doctor both shot him looks that shut him up, and fast.

"I guess if you look at my mother's life, you can see that she's a good woman who doesn't always do good things. I don't know if she doesn't understand that she hurts people or if she just can't help herself."

"That's the key, of course," April said.

"Knowing *why* she does it?" Kurt asked.

"No, knowing that only *she* can help herself. You can't fix your mother, Kurt. Just like I can't—"

"Oh, don't even finish that sentence, honey. No one can fix your daddy!" Dr. Joyce roared, laughing as she descended the steps and walked to her car.

Kurt met April's gaze and instantly knew. She hadn't intended to say "I can't fix my daddy."

Just what she felt so much sorrow about not being able to fix, though, would remain a mystery for now. The sun had begun to set, the doctor was heading home and he needed to make sure Miss Cora and April had what they needed before he could do the same.

"Looks like instead of me moving in today, you are." April would live in his new home before he did. It didn't irritate him nearly as much as he thought it might. "Can I run by your apartment and get you anything?"

Her lips formed a silent "Oh." Her gaze shifted right, then left, then out to his truck. "What did you bring for yourself?"

"I don't know. Some food. Toiletries. T-shirts and jeans."

"I'll take the food, toiletries and a T-shirt for now, thanks." She made her way to the front door.

"Okay, I get wanting to eat and clean up, but why do you want one of my T-shirts?"

"Because, silly—" she looked back over her shoulder at him, not a hint of guile in her eyes "—I have to sleep in something."

Guile or not, Kurt felt sucker punched at the very image of April wearing his shirt to sleep in. He dragged in a deep breath of cool, end-of-winter air and said, "Maybe when the doctor volunteered to bring out a cotton gown for Miss Cora, you should have asked for one for yourself."

"I didn't actually realize I'd be staying here." She turned so that she stood poised on the threshold, her back to him and both of them gazing down the hallway into the grand old home. "It is *your* house, after all."

"Yes, but Miss Cora is *your* guest here. Besides, there is not a chance in—"

"Language." She dipped her head and gave him a sidelong glance, her finger to her lips. "There's a ninety-year-old in the house, you know."

She looked so wonderful there like that. Tempting but not by design, and sweet but not like some syrupy act.

"There is not one chance in a million that Miss Cora

would let me check to see how her bruises were healing, much less help with her personal care." He shifted his weight. "So looks like you've got the honors and the run of the household for the next one or two—"

"Or four, or…" she interrupted, quoting the doctor's timetable with a smile.

He rolled his eyes. "Or six, or—"

"So," she said softly.

"Or so days," he concluded, unable to take his eyes from her. "Will you be all right out here?"

"If I have any trouble, I'll know who to call."

"Yeah?"

"Yeah. Miss Cora has informed me she used to be pretty handy with a gun."

He laughed, stopped to think if there were any firearms on the property and then, confident there weren't, laughed again. "Okay, big funny. If you have even a hint of trouble with anything—wild animals, stuck pickle jars, lady-eating dogwood trees—you call me, you hear?"

"I hear you, Kurt." She stepped inside, then looked at him through the rusted screen of the closed door. "And while I do appreciate your offer, rest assured, I am not going to *need* you to come to my rescue. Not now. Or ever."

Chapter Six

Into the lion's den.

Kurt wouldn't presume to compare himself to a true hero of the Bible. In fact, during the one night, since being out at the house with April and Miss Cora, as he'd tossed and turned on the couch in his half-packed-up apartment, he had come to suspect that heroism might be downright unachievable for a guy like him.

How could he ever be a hero when he'd shown such weakness in the past?

No, Kurt didn't see himself as Danielesque in any way. But he couldn't resist imagining the women on the other side of that door as ready to pounce on him and have him for lunch.

Or, at least, as an appetizer for the lunch they'd already planned.

Well, a man had to do what he had to do. And

since running off to Ezra's Holler to keep himself out
of harm's—and the Council of Christian Women's—
way was now an impossibility, he had decided to
meet the situation head-on. Nip it in the bud. Show
them he was the captain of his own fate, not a man
to be manipulated.

He just hoped his mama wasn't inside.

He wasn't scared of his mama. He respected her.
And loved her. But he cringed whenever she opened
her mouth. So whenever he found himself in situations where her mouth could prove to be a potential
land mine, as it were, he made careful preparations
and a few quick prayers for patience, restraint and
selective hearing.

He remained standing outside the large, swinging
double doors and took a deep breath. He could do this.

A lifetime of training had certainly taught him
one thing at least. *Sometimes the only way to gain
the upper hand with a crafty, committed opponent
was...*

He pushed the doors wide open, took command
of the room with one sweeping gaze and kept his
tone low as he said, "Hello, ladies. Don't you all look
lovely today."

To utilize the element of charm.

It was a weapon he rarely had any use for. But to
protect April from the cutting tongues and kindest
intentions of her closest friends and family, he would
gladly pour it on, and thick.

Toward that end, he did not move into the room immediately but stood in the doorway, making a point to survey the clusters of women seated at half a dozen white linen-covered tables. "C'mon, ladies, take the bait," he murmured under his breath, through that smile that he'd been told made him look like he had a slightly wicked secret.

Heads turned. A murmur moved through the room from those nearest him all the way to the water pitchers and coffeepot set up against the back wall. All eyes were fixed on him in his freshly pressed uniform.

A coo here.

A giggle there.

Kurt did not have a vain bone in his body, but he knew the score around town. Over forty but still fit, he was educated, armed and unattached, old money. Moonie had not exaggerated when he suggested that a lot of women considered the unattached part of the equation an outright challenge.

There were single women around town who wanted to be married women, after all. Women who *should* be married. Women who deserved to be wives and, if the Lord saw fit to bless them in that way, mothers. With lots of babies. Women just waiting to love and be loved. And there *he* was, perfectly good husband and father material going to waste.

Except, of course, he knew better. He was lousy

husband material. Though he'd have liked to have been a father, he was old school enough to believe that the husband part came first. You loved someone, built a foundation and a home with them, and then brought a child into the world out of your love for each other. Being a father meant marriage, and he wasn't going there again.

Which was precisely why he had to come *here*.

Owtt's Eatery. *The* restaurant in Wileyville. Not the premiere restaurant. Not the classiest restaurant. The only restaurant.

Oh, yeah, there was a diner. Nice-enough place to grab a sandwich and chips. And the Not by Bread Alone Bakery for breakfast and coffee. But for a real dining experience—or for any group meet-and-eat—Owtt's was the place. Usually.

He nodded in greeting to Claudia Addams, current president of his collective nemesis, the Council of Christian Women, who sat at a dais. He smiled and said, "I see you ladies have moved on from meeting in the cemetery."

"Oh, we finished that beautification project weeks ago." Claudia motioned for him. "Come on in and join us, Sheriff. We'd love to have you as our guest today, if you can stay."

She tilted her head, which made her bright-gold earrings glint against her dark skin. When she smiled his way, she did not show her teeth.

He tried to read something into that smile. Had

she beckoned him inside to join them because she sincerely wanted him there? Or was she just going through the motions of hospitality? Or maybe she was just trying to get him to wade into their ranks in order to make him an easier target?

"We'd love to tell you all about our current project," she said. "See how we can factor you into the mix, as it were."

That answered his questions. *Target.* She had definitely lured him inside to make him a better target for the women bound and determined to do him good. At least, she didn't hem and haw and demur about it. He should have expected the direct approach from the wife of a distinguished senior minister.

"You may be disappointed, ma'am. I don't tend to mix well with others."

"Not to worry!" She shook her head, smiling now with all her teeth, both cheeks and her eyes. "We can attend to the mixing up of things like you wouldn't believe."

"I've heard that rumor." He laughed despite his tightening chest. So much for showing them he was the captain of his own fate. He might just be out manned here.

"Rumor? What rumor?" A familiar voice came from just beyond his right shoulder.

Outmanned *and* outmaneuvered.

"Hello, Mama." Kurt turned to plant a kiss on

his mother's forehead. The aroma of the hot rolls on the plate in her hand rose to fill his nostrils. "Those for me?"

"Stick around," she said in the way only mamas of the no-nonsense variety could. "You'll get what's coming to you all in good time."

"Ha!" Another voice carried from across the room, growing louder as the speaker approached. "I've been saying that for years, that one day he'd get what's coming to him. But here the man stands before us, still single and childless, not a love handle or paunch on him, and empowered with the ability to throw anyone who gets on his very last nerve in jail."

He stiffened. "If that last part were true…"

"Stop it." His mother patted his cheek and jerked her white head toward the cumbersomely pregnant woman who'd joined them. "Kiss your sister."

He minded his mama. He always felt obliged to mind his mama—at least whenever she was around. Which explained why he spent so many years *not* being around, traveling the world with the army.

"Your time is coming, Brother, trust me," Kurt's sister, Pat, said.

"Yours, too." He rubbed her belly and laughed.

"Two more weeks," she said.

"Two weeks? That for me or you?"

She looked at the women stealing glimpses his way and warned him in hushed tones, "Oh, I don't think *you'll* make it as long as two weeks."

"Do they plan to marry me or bury me?"

"Dum-dum-da-dum." She sounded out the opening to "The Wedding March."

"Here comes the bride and there goes the groom. I am not staying around and letting them overrun my life for the next two weeks." He helped his sister into a chair and, while leaning to get her settled, whispered in her ear, "If you have a better idea about how to get them off my back, speak now or forever hold your—"

"Sweet tea?"

It sounded like April. Same general quality. Same accent.

Same impeccable timing for catching him mid-thought and making him rethink everything.

Kurt straightened and turned to meet the inevitable. "Hello, Sadie," he said, greeting April's sister.

In his big plan to confront the enemy on their own turf, he hadn't counted on a secret weapon.

Sadie Shelnutt Pickett. April's younger sister and the only person in town who had actually caught on to Kurt's and April's secret, short-lived not-quite romance.

Kurt made his excuse to sister and, with a jerk of his head, directed Sadie to join him at an empty table away from the group. "You have something to say to me, Sadie?"

"No. Nothing in particular. I heard you just *happened by* when Miss Cora took to feeling poorly out at Ezra's Holler." She poured iced tea into one of the tall glasses circling the unoccupied table.

"Okay." He plunked his elbows down, one hand dangling over the edge of the table. "Spill it."

She set the glass of icy liquid in front of him, her gaze just as chilled but anything but refreshing. "Don't tempt me, Sheriff."

He moved the glass aside. "Tell me everything you know about what went on out at Ezra's Holler yesterday."

She poured herself a glass and made a show of shrugging as if the whole subject bored her to tears. "What's to know?"

He narrowed his eyes at the woman with hair as curly as April's was straight. "I asked you first."

She rattled the ice-filled pitcher in his direction.

He didn't even flinch.

"Okay." She set the pitcher down and wriggled into her seat as if she needed to plant herself for a long gab session. "About half an hour after April was supposed to open her shop this morning, my phone rang."

"April called?" he asked.

"Everybody *but* April." She took a sip of her iced tea, then continued, picking up speed as she did. "All saying things like 'Where's April?' 'Is April okay?' 'She's not at the shop or answering the door at her apartment.' Of course, I was…"

He leaned closer. "Alarmed?"

She leaned closer, putting herself six inches away from his nose. "Cautiously optimistic."

He sat back. "Optimistic? About April going missing?"

She shook her head and sat back. "About April going missing around the same time that our adorable, single sheriff loaded up his pickup truck like a man getting ready to start a new life."

He closed his eyes. "Can a person do anything in this town without someone noticing it and sending out an APB?"

"Oh, relax, will you?" She nudged his shin under the table with the toe of her tennis shoe. "Daddy told me about how he put the fear of God-honoring women into you with his little talk about the Easter benevolence program, so I'd gone by to have a word with you and saw you drive off. I didn't tell anyone."

"Not even about being cautiously optimistic?"

"Nope." She made the sign for her lips being sealed.

He nodded his thanks. "Okay, so that's established. But what did you mean by saying you were cautiously optimistic, anyway?"

"Hey, you and my sister leave town at the same time, a pickup packed up and ready to start a new life... I thought maybe dating wasn't the only thing you two might try to do in secret." She pointed to the ring on her left hand.

He tried to swallow. He clenched his jaw. This

was exactly what he'd wanted to protect April from. Wild speculation, unrealistic expectations, gossip, rumors, disappointment.

He lowered his voice and honed his gaze on the one person who could set this horrible sequence in motion, or stop it. "You made the leap from watching me drive away with some boxes in the truck—and my dog, I might add—to me running off and eloping with your sister?"

"Hey, you've known me since high school. I'm really good at leaping. In fact, I've never let not knowing what's going on stand in the way of a great leap."

He scowled. "Who'd have thought that Sadie Pickett and Lollie Muldoon would have so much in common?"

"Hey, that's not nice. I didn't *tell* anybody what I saw or what I hoped or what I leapt into." She paused, then scrunched up her nose at the way that had come out.

He did manage a chuckle. "That should teach you to be more careful about all that leaping. It could land you in a heap of hurt, you know."

"That's why I kept it to myself. You think you're the only person in this town influenced by the actions of a, um, high-profile parent? Believe me, I know what it's like to hear your name followed by a bunch of laughter in the fellowship hall after church."

"Laughter. That's tough, too, I suppose." Personally, he'd encountered eyes that darted away from his, sentences that cut off whenever he entered the room, awkward sympathy to his face and a knife sticking out of his back ready to be twisted by some well-meaning well-wisher. "But April never seems all that bothered by Moonie's antics, you know?"

"No. She sort of enjoys them, I think. Maybe because she's so closed off, she gets a vicarious kick out of him pulling all those stunts, like marching with the children in the Memorial Day parade or riding around town on a lawn mower with the flag flying from the back." She looked into her glass and sighed. "Actually, I think April and Daddy were a great team."

"Team?"

"He created the distractions while she worked tirelessly behind the scenes to make sure no one dug up the truth."

"About your mother's depression and your father bringing you and your sisters here to keep you from being taken away from him by social services?"

"Yeah. Of course, now that everybody and their sheriff knows that story, April doesn't have much of a role to play on the team anymore."

Even if the role existed, she wouldn't want it anymore. Kurt understood that now. Which brought him back to his reason for coming today. "So what do people think about April?"

"They like her. A lot. I think you'd agree with them if you'd only give her a—"

He held his hand up to cut her off. "What do they think about her being gone?"

Sadie cocked her head. "What's *to* think?"

"Then they aren't talking about it?"

"No, I'm asking what's to think? Obviously, there's a better story there than what April told me when I finally got her on her cellphone, and it sounds like you're privy to it, pal."

"If you are really my pal, you won't press me for details, Sadie."

"Okay, just promise me that my sister isn't going to get hurt."

"I promise I will do everything in my power to shelter April, to protect her from..." Myself. He couldn't make promises about other things hurting her, though. "You know, you never told me what's being said about April not being there to open her store."

"What's to be said? Miss Cora asked April to take her out to Ezra's Holler and they're staying a few days." She relaxed, looked around the room, gave a friendly wave to someone, then a more-insistent don't-come-over-here wave before looking him in the eye again. "It's exactly the kind of charity the COCW wants to encourage with the benevolence program. In fact, several ladies offered to go out there, but April said it would be unsettling for Miss Cora because she just wouldn't be able to be a fitting hostess to them."

He thought of the old gal trying to serve tea and finger sandwiches, lying on her side with pillows stacked against her behind. Not a fitting hostess. That certainly wasn't a lie.

"So we've decided to take turns keeping the store running while April's out there."

Knowing his mama was within earshot and probably had her hearing aid turned on high in hopes of picking up anything being said here, he cleared his throat before speaking and said only, "That's mighty nice of the ladies."

"Well, there are a lot of mighty nice ladies in this town."

"So your father tells me."

"You know he's mostly hot air and nonsense, don't you?"

"You saying the COCW won't try to marry me off as a public-service project between now and Easter?"

"No, I can't honestly say they won't. But I don't see what you can do about it." She raised her glass and, while taking a long drink, peered over the rim at one table of women, then the next.

"Obviously, I was going to leave town, but with Miss Cora, uh, waylaid and Dr. Joyce volunteering me to run errands for her, that isn't an option anymore."

"So what are your options then?"

"I only see one."

"One." She mouthed the word as much as said it, then shook her head in what he had long ago recognized as the international code of women for "Men! They just don't get anything."

He cleared his throat and tugged his collar solidly into place. "I plan to confront the ladies of the COCW and tell them, in no uncertain terms, that I am off-limits, off the market—"

"Off your rocker?" She gave her glass a wobble and the ice cracked and clinked in it.

"Huh?"

"You can try dealing with them that way, but I think you're making a big mistake."

He grinned. "You think the church ladies of the COCW will get the best of me?"

She set the glass on the table with a solid clunk. "No, I honestly don't think any woman is going to get the best of you, Kurt. Not until you find the best in yourself to give."

He picked up his glass and took a sip. "Deep."

She smiled and primped for him. "I have my moments."

"No, I meant it's getting deep in here—reminds me of my days mucking out horse stalls as a kid."

"For that, I have half a mind not to tell you how to remove yourself from the clutches of the crafty women of the benevolence program."

"You've presented me with quite a dilemma there, Sadie."

"Can't decide whether to go on with your own ill-conceived, doomed-to-failure, clearly inferior plan or apologize to me and avail yourself of my brilliant, well-thought-out, obviously superior scheme?"

"No. I can't decide whether to make a crack about you having half a mind for thinking you can help me out of this mess or admitting that I have half a mind for actually sitting here considering taking your advice."

"Take my advice, Kurt. *Take* my advice."

"Okay, shoot."

"Hopefully, it won't go so far as to require gunplay," she teased. She took a deep breath, adjusted in her chair again, waved off another someone wanting to approach and then leaned close to whisper her great idea. "Fight fire with fire."

"When they start coming at me with marriage matches, I wave torches at them like the villagers in the old black-and-white monster movies?"

She laughed. "How about if you can't beat them, join them?"

"Join them? The COCW? Okay, but I'm not putting on a fancy dress and riding on the parade float y'all sponsor every Christmas."

"Ha-ha." She narrowed her eyes at him in the only warning she gave before launching into a full explanation. "How about if you don't give them a chance to make a project out of you?"

"How do I do that? Or how do I *not* do that?"

"You—" she stabbed her finger in his direction to make her point "—make a project out of someone else."

His gut knotted, but he had to say it. "April and Miss Cora?"

"Of course." She held her hand out, palm up. "You're already checking in on them."

"This is like one of those reality shows where cameras follow me around everywhere and I'm the only one who doesn't know it, right?" He pretended to search the premises for the offending hidden lens.

"No." She smacked him lightly on the arm. "This is like a town where people care about one another and where the administrator of Miss Cora's assisted-living center called to ask if I'd take some of the old gal's clothes out when I went to see April."

He dropped the humor, his throat tight. "You're going to see April?"

"Not if there is someone else already seeing to everything she needs."

He rubbed his forehead with two fingertips, relieved but reassured by the idea. "Me."

"Yeah."

"And that will keep the COCW off my back?"

"As long as you're occupied with your own project, they have to. Think about it. How could they do something to detract you from your own service by imposing their idea of how to help you on you?"

"I hear you talking, but I'm not sure you actually *said* anything." He pressed the heel of his hand to his temple and shook his head. "And if I did hear you right, I'm not sure that your sister will like being considered a project."

"Then again, she might like being part of a team again."

"Team?"

"She provides the distraction—"

"While I try to keep the truth hidden."

"That is what this is all about, isn't it, Kurt? You have some truth in you, about you, that you don't want everyone in Wileyville to know?"

"I think everyone in Wileyville *does* know, Sadie. That's the problem."

And what are you going to do about it?

He raised his head to take in their surroundings. Each time his gaze met someone else's, the woman looked away. Some put their heads together and whispered. Other tablemates exchanged knowing glances. His sister shook her head as if to tell him he wasn't fooling anyone. Their mother fixed him with her empathetic Mommy-only-wants-the-best-for-you expression. The second Lollie was absorbed in intimate conversation, Pat snatched up her white cloth napkin, held it to her head like a wedding veil and pointed directly at him.

He ran his hand through his hair, knowing he'd

hear about it later from his mother, and sighed. "I can't. I can't stand here and talk about your sister behind her back to these people."

"Then go." She tilted her head toward the door. "I'll do it."

He hesitated. "Isn't that the coward's way out?"

"Go," she assured him.

He stood. "I don't know how I'll ever convince your sister that this was the lesser of two evils."

"Convince? Convince who? You don't mean you're going to tell her about it, do you?"

"Well, yeah, I think I owe her that much."

"Off. Your. Rocker." She said each word slow and hard and added the "Men don't get it" headshake for good measure. "If you tell her, she will turn around and tell everyone it's not true and then where will you be?"

"I, uh—"

"Filling out your date book with the names of all the blind dates and not-so-secret setups. That's where you'll be, my friend."

"But I can't keep that kind of thing from April. It's deceitful."

She sighed and gazed up at him all doe-eyed and gooey. "Are you really sure you are off-limits for matchmaking because I know this girl—"

"Sadie, you're making Plan A look better and better all the time."

"Is Plan A where you tell the ladies to back off

because my reaction was intended to show you how much your reticence will only make them want to charge in and get involved all the more."

"No, Plan A is where I head for the hills until the coast is clear."

"Oh. Well, you *could* do that."

"Except I can't."

"Because you made a promise?"

"Yeah." That and he had two women staying in his private getaway that nobody knew *was* his private getaway, and if he left them in the lurch, then all kinds of people would *invade* his private getaway and, no matter what, Kurt was stuck.

And stuck good.

"I am not going to announce to all of Wileyville that I have taken on the local old maids as my benevolence project for the season, Sadie."

"Then go. I will say something. Not that, but something."

"You *have* to tell the truth."

"And *you* have to keep the truth to yourself."

"Not to worry. I've gotten to be an old hand at that." He was in the fix he was in because of it. And because he was a man who wanted to keep his business to himself, he'd just keep right on doing that and let April's sister handle the rest.

He leaned down and gave Sadie a pat on the back. "Thanks."

"No problem." She waved goodbye. "Go."

He tipped his head to the group. "Ladies! Enjoy your lunches."

They murmured goodbyes.

"Call me later, hon," his mama hollered, good and loud for all to hear.

He gave an obedient salute.

Pat plucked the silk flowers from the vase at the center of the table and held them like a bridal bouquet.

He rolled his eyes. His only regret? He wouldn't be in the room to sneer at his sister in good fun when Sadie announced the plan to undo all matchmaking plans.

One last wave and he was out the door.

Done.

And he had remained true to his vow to never talk about someone he cared for to others.

He had to feel good about that. Didn't he?

Behind closed doors, he knew it was Sadie banging a spoon against a glass.

It grew quiet. Or as quiet as the COCW ever could be.

"Okay, ladies," Sadie began. "Everyone with 'Find Kurt Muldoon a nice girl' on your list of potential good deeds to get done by Easter, strike it off right now."

A murmur built in the room and Kurt could imagine their crestfallen faces. What he couldn't imagine was what Sadie would say next. He heard the tapping of the glass again, then Sadie's very loud, very self-assured voice add "I've just taken care of that myself."

Chapter Seven

"Forgive him. Forgive him not." Dried leaves and branches crackled with every handful April yanked from the long, untended patch of once-lush garden.

She came outside shortly after lunch, when Miss Cora demurely mumbled something about having a fitful night—which April took to mean she kept rolling over onto her tender backside and waking herself up—and returned to the bedroom to try to take a nap. April considered doing the same, but really, she wasn't sleepy. Or, rather, she wasn't likely to get any sleep. Not lying in a bed in a home that she couldn't help thinking, under more favorable circumstances, might have been her own.

Her own home. With Kurt. At Ezra's Holler. Sweet, serene, secluded Ezra's Holler. *With Kurt.*

If only every single thing about their lives had been different.

So she came outside wanting to escape.

First, onto the wide porch, where the rusting hooks in the ceiling made her think of sharing a porch swing in the arms of a certain man on spring afternoons.

Then, out into the yard, where she could see the cabins across the way and practically hear the laughing, rowdy families rolling up with loaded cars for summer vacations. Kids splashing in the pond. Moms calling them in for supper. Dads snoring in the hammocks.

All reminders of moments she'd never have. Not just never have but moments she'd never even witness firsthand.

Finally, out to the quarter acre of land that now seemed like nothing more than a mass of dead plants surrounded by a crumbling, waist-high wall. But she knew better. There was life here still. Clear away all that did not belong here, all that kept new life from springing forth, and this place would surprise you. If someone would care just a little and tend to it, this place would bloom.

She hadn't planned on diving in and attacking the worst of the overgrowth. She shouldn't be doing any gardening at all. For starters, she didn't have a change of clothes.

As if she needed to illustrate her point, she wiped her hand along her pant leg, leaving a streak of dirt.

And she was wearing Kurt's T-shirt.

She tugged at the knot she had made in the hem

to keep the shirt from snagging on branches as she pushed her way through the remains of the pathway that ended at a broken fountain in a circle in the garden's center.

Besides, Kurt had told her he didn't require any help taking care of the landscaping.

She swatted back some stray hair that was tickling her cheek and neck.

But since she was here and restless…

"Forgive him." Up came a nasty-looking thorn-covered shoot and then another. "Forgive him not."

She decided that spending a few hours wearing herself out doing something productive might just take the edge off. She bent down to grab a withered stalk of pokeweed by its base and gave it a yank. It broke off with enough kickback that her hand flew back and brittle bits nested in her braid. That would be a mess to get out, but she didn't care.

"Forgive him. Forgive—" she took a deep breath and concluded "—forgive him."

She had to do it. She had to find a way. Clearly, the man had not set out to hurt and humiliate her. He had always been up-front about what he wanted: a few discreet dates now and then.

Dinners—out of town only.

Someone to talk to on the phone each evening after work.

A companion to go for a drive in the country.

Someone to make him laugh and never try to make him be something he could not be.

No ties.

No public displays of any kind.

No…

She couldn't say no future. In fact, that was the reason she felt the most cheated, the most conflicted. Kurt had wanted a future with her.

His vision of the future.

A relationship, she supposed, that wouldn't have looked all that much different than this neglected garden. There would be life in it but unseen, untended, slowly stifling itself to death but never quite dying out completely.

If April wanted more, she'd have to find it somewhere else.

But she was over forty and hadn't found it somewhere else. What were the odds of her walking away from the one decent grown-up guy in Wileyville, Kentucky, who didn't think himself the prize catch of the universe and finding someone new? With every unattached female from last year's eighteen-year-old Dogwood Blossom Queen to Miss Cora splashing around in the same dating pool? April was more likely to drown in that pool than find another guy as right for her as…as the one that got away.

Kurt had counted on that very insecurity to keep her from walking out on the little bit of relationship he was willing to give. He'd exploited her vulnerability to get his way.

And the situation might have remained unchanged if she hadn't learned the harsh truth about her mother's death, why she had sent her children and husband away and how keeping secrets had kept them from becoming as close and loving as they could have been. She thought of all the wasted years when she and her sisters had bickered rather than bonded because each of them had let their fears and questions about their missing mother stand between them. She'd made the decision that she would not keep secrets anymore. She would step out into the light, warts and all, and encourage others to do the same. To talk. To share.

"To forgive," she whispered.

She *had* to forgive Kurt.

She glanced down at the dried-up, crushed leaves in her hand. She pressed her lips closed tight. Her throat constricted. Dampness bathed her eyes, and a tear rolled down her cheek. Without thinking, she reached up to wipe the wetness away and ended up swiping the debris in her hand alongside her head.

"Careful now, you're getting brambles in your pretty braid!"

"Me? Miss Cora, you're the one who should be careful." April got to her feet and rushed forward to offer support to the elderly woman toddling awkwardly toward her, wielding a cane and using her pocketbook for counterbalance. "Walking out here all by yourself."

"Walking I can do. Doctor's orders. It's sitting that gives me fits, girl. And, besides, a person's never alone in a garden. You, of all people, should know that." She leaned on her cane and began to hum the hymn "In the Garden." "I saw you out here tangling with this dried-up jungle of sticks and branches and decided to come out and help with the brush."

"Miss Cora, I can't let you help clear away—"

"Not *that* brush, *this* brush!" She withdrew a wooden hairbrush from her pocketbook. "Come sit on this concrete bench over here and let me get the tangles and stickers out of that braid of yours. Then I'll lend you the scarf I have in my pocketbook for protection."

"Miss Cora, I can't let you—"

"Let me? Indulge me. I used to do this kind of thing for my mother. Sit out here and comb through her pretty, long hair. I'd love to do it for you."

Miss Cora motioned to the bench, and when April relented by sitting, the older woman began to tug the band on her braid loose. "It's no insignificant thing that the Bible shows us how events that shaped God's relationship with His children took place in gardens—Eden, Gethsemane."

"You going to quiz me on how much I remember from Sunday school classes, Miss Cora?"

"Darlin', if you don't know what happened in

Eden and Gethsemane, then I might well have taught badminton classes instead of the Bible."

"Oh, I bet you'd have been cute as a bug in a bad-minton outfit chasing down birdies with a racquet."

"If I recall the way most of my classes went back when you were young, I'd have done better to have chased a few of you young ones with something. Lollie's boy, for one. Now there was a boy who didn't think he needed anyone to tell him anything."

"He hasn't changed."

"Everything changes, April. Gardens remind us of that more than most things we run across in our lives. They are always in a state of change, of growth and struggling to survive, of blossoming and beauty, of death and falling away, of coming alive again." She shook the strands of the braid apart gently, then paused. "This garden used to be magnificent."

April's shoulders slumped a bit, and she tried to picture how the garden must have been when Cora was a child. "I guess you spent a lot of hours out here, working and weeding."

"Uh-huh. And my mother before me. My father, now his interest lay in planting the seeds of a strong community. A church, a school, some homes, a jailhouse."

"I think if we are still here tomorrow, Miss Cora, I'd like to explore the grounds, if you don't mind."

"Not my place to mind. I don't own this land or anything on it anymore. The old school, the jail, the springhouse—those I sold with the property to Lollie's boy, so I suppose it's him you'd have to ask for permission."

"Oh, we probably won't be seeing him out here again before we go back to town."

"Why not? What's wrong with that boy anyway?"

"Wrong?"

"Not wrong like peculiar. Wrong like, well, like something ails him. A kind of hurt, an inside hurt, you know what I mean?"

"Yes, I know what you mean. But as for Kurt, I don't know what ails him. Can anyone ever really know what kind of hurt someone else is carrying around inside? Unless the other person opens up, that is."

"He can't fool me. I might not have the best eyesight, but when it comes to the inner seeing of things, I'm not blind, you know."

April's smile quickly changed to a wince. The old gal might have a certain insight about human beings, but she didn't seem to have a clue how to use a hairbrush. "Miss Cora? I—"

"You don't have to confess a thing, young lady."

"Confess?"

"I know you got a hurt inside of you, too."

"Actually, right now I'm more concerned about the hurt *outside* of me." She pressed her hand to her scalp. "But thank you for your concern. You're the first person who ever seemed to notice that about me."

"Not the first, I don't think."

"Okay, my family did, when everything about our whole history exploded in our faces."

"Oh, family." Cora huffed and worked the brush loose. "They're the last ones who see who we really are, I think, even when you're standing right before them your entire lifetime."

It sounded as if Miss Cora had a bit of unresolved hurt in her, as well.

April patted her hand. "Matter of not seeing the forest for the family tree, I suppose."

"Forest? Family tree?" Miss Cora cackled lightly. "You're quick with those, girl."

"Thank you."

"So let me throw one of my own your way."

"Uh, okay."

"That hurt in you? It's like the dead limbs on the dogwood tree outside my window."

April tensed.

"And you, being a gardener and all, you know deadwood doesn't blossom. It has to be cleared away. God gives us winter so we can appreciate the spring."

"You teaching Sunday school or botany class, Miss Cora?"

"I'm teaching truth, girl. People are no different than God's other creations. He tells us as much. 'Consider the lilies of the field, how they grow. They toil not. Neither do they spin. And yet I say unto you, that even Solomon in all his glory was not arrayed like one of these.'"

"Bet you can still tell me chapter and verse on that." April marveled at the recall the woman had over the Bible.

"Matthew 6:28 and 6:29." Miss Cora tapped April on the shoulder with the side of the hairbrush as if she could somehow hammer the lesson in at last. "And just like the lilies and the dogwood, we have to clear away all that is no longer useful to us before the Lord can really begin to work in us and help us bloom."

April drew in a deep breath. It was cool still, and the air stung going in. But not as much as Miss Cora's next words.

"You do *want* to bloom, don't you, dear?"

"Of course!" she said, a bit too forcefully.

"Good. Because sometimes, some of us would rather hang on to a lifeless limb than let it fall away and see what God will bring us in its place."

Was Miss Cora talking about April or herself?

"I'm not just talking about *you* now, you know."

"Ah." April glanced back over her shoulder at the woman's sweet, smiling face. "I didn't think so."

"I'm talking about Lollie's boy, as well." She began the brushing again without even looking where the bristles landed.

"K-Kurt?" April jerked to avoid taking a brush to the side of the head. "You're talking about Kurt?"

"Yes, and the hurt he carries inside that he won't shed himself of." She dug into the task of brushing hair with such gusto that April half imagined the old gal digging her heels into the soft ground to get better leverage. "Leaves me with the idea that maybe the pair of you could—"

"Stop!"

The hairbrush stilled.

Miss Cora kept right on talking. "With a little time and willingness on both your parts to—"

"Miss Cora, I didn't mean to stop brushing." Though April was pretty grateful for the reprieve. "I meant stop right there trying to get Kurt Muldoon and me coupled off. It just isn't going to happen."

"Don't you like him? I thought I saw that you liked him in your eyes, girl."

"But that's not—"

"And I sure can see he likes you."

"Really?" No. Don't go there, she warned herself. "It doesn't matter, Miss Cora. We can *like* each other. We could even *love* each other, but it wouldn't work between us."

"Because of that hurt inside you. Yes, I can see how that would create a barrier. But if you would both just clear away that useless stuff, I know that you could—"

"Blossom into romance?" She didn't know if the elderly woman would pick up on the bitterness and sarcasm in her tone and, by this point, she did not care.

"Stop fighting this." Miss Cora took up the brush again. "And let me finish the job."

Cool fingertips plucked a twig from behind April's ear, then sank the bristles into the back of April's neck.

Her back went rigid. All thoughts of trying to lay the blame for their lack of a relationship on Kurt disappeared. All April wanted now was to survive Miss Cora's kindness, then get back to yanking up overgrowth to vent her feelings about the man in question.

"I always dreamt of having a girl, a daughter, to brush her hair and talk with her in this garden. Did your mother ever sit with you like this?"

"My mother…" April took a deep breath. What was the point in explaining? Even if she could get Miss Cora to understand about her mother, she couldn't get her to remember what had been said a day from now. "No, ma'am."

"That's too bad."

"Yes, ma'am. It is." It was. She hadn't had a mother, really. Another in the long list of things-most-people-take-for-granted-in-life that April lacked. She didn't feel sad about it, though. She'd had a wonderful life so far, blessed by God in so many ways. And by grace, given an opportunity to sort out all the issues that had nagged at her for so long.

Except the very thing that had driven her out into this disused plot of lost potential in the first place: figuring out how to forgive Kurt.

"Close your eyes, girl, and relax."

"I'll close my eyes," she muttered under her breath. "But I can't promise to relax."

"That's just fine," the spry senior said in a suspiciously sweet tone. "Just keep them peepers closed and let—"

"What was that?" April started to turn her head toward the sound.

"What?" Cora grabbed April's chin and pointed her face so that all April could see was the back of the vacant schoolhouse in the distance—and all Cora could see was the back of her head.

"I thought I heard a… *Ow!*" April reached around to bury her fingers in her hair, or where she hoped she still had hair after Miss Cora's particularly brisk attack on a pokeweed-produced snarl.

Again, Cora set her head so she could only see straight ahead. "It wouldn't hurt if you'd sit still."

"But I—"

"Close your eyes."

"Miss Cora, I—"

"Close 'em. And while you're at it, zip those lips, too, Missy. I didn't come out here to listen to a bunch of back talk."

"Yes, ma'am." She closed her eyes and set her mouth in a thin line. It would only hurt for a few minutes and then…

Then Miss Cora began singing her favorite hymn at the top of her lungs. "I come to the garden alone…"

The brush went downward, snagging.

"Come on, girl, you know this one. Sing it with me."

April managed to mumble a line, gulped in some air and cringed, preparing for the next assault to her scalp.

A crunch of dried grass underfoot.

Miss Cora's voice raised louder still.

April almost worked up the nerve to open her eyes. Well, one eye. Just a slit.

And then the brush went gliding from the crown to the ends of her hair in one long, smooth stroke.

April waited until a second stroke proved it hadn't been a fluke, then exhaled, long and soft, and gave herself over to the soothing sensation. "That's nice."

"Yeah, it is." He spoke softly, so softly she scarcely heard him.

She supposed she should have jumped up, startled half out of her wits, but instead she smiled. She had heard the car drive up, after all, and even though she wasn't a worldly woman regarding men, she could sense the difference when a six-foot-something brawny specimen was standing beside her instead of the slip of a lady who had been there moments before.

"It's chilly out here. I'm going in to fix some tea. Y'all come along when you're ready. Don't mind me." Cora toddled off toward the house.

"Should I walk her back?" Kurt asked.

"No. As she already reminded me, Dr. Joyce says she needs the exercise to keep from stiffening up. Her legs might be thin as twigs, but they aren't going to give out on her."

"Okay, then, I'll stay and finish the job she put me to." He whisked a leaf from her upper arm.

She shivered.

"Big joke, huh? Trying to fool me by trading places with Miss Cora?" she asked.

"I wasn't trying to fool you, April." He gathered her hair in one hand and let it fall against her back again. "Ever."

"Oh?"

He leaned down, both hands on her shoulders, and spoke into one ear. "I just walked up because I— I was thinking I might have something to tell you, something you might want to know. But as soon as I got here, Miss Cora held the brush out to me and, well, I figured if I didn't take it, she'd chase me around the garden and use it on my backside."

"Is it important?"

"My backside? Well, not to the average person, but I'm kind of attached to it." He grinned.

She was a puddle. The man had brushed her hair, touched her arm, made a cornball joke and she had melted. Melted, which was not the same as moved on…or made peace with…or forgiven him.

"What you thought you might want to tell me…is it important?" She turned her head slightly and found herself staring directly into his eyes. His deep, kind, searching green eyes.

"I don't know. See, I went to talk to the ladies at the COCW and—"

"The COCW?" *Ugh!* "I already fended them off once today."

Kept them from coming out here and overwhelming her with virtuous intentions and voracious questions, she had.

"Don't get me wrong. I love those ladies. Love them dearly. But…" But for once in a very long time, she managed to escape the meeting, the obligations and, most of all, the sad, sincere gazes of her sisters in Christ that all seemed to say "Poor April, poor, unloved, unwanted April," and she was not going to let him drag her back into the guilt trap by telling her what they had to say.

"But you'd rather not bring them out here in body or in spirit, I gather?"

"Please. Grant me that. Just while I'm here, no talk about the COCW and whatever they are up to." She held up her hand. "I'm sure whatever it is, I'll learn about it all in good time. Unless—unless you really think I should know this very minute."

"This *very* minute?"

"Uh-huh."

"Actually, there are other things I'd rather do this *very* minute." He studied her for a moment in complete and utter silence.

She swallowed, blinked and tried to look away but couldn't. She drew in a deep breath of air scented with dried grass and aftershave and jumped headlong into small talk. "How'd you know where to find us?"

"Are you kidding? When I found that my favorite houseguests weren't inside, I knew just where you would be."

"Even though you told me you didn't need me to do anything with this garden?"

"*Especially* because I told you that."

"I couldn't help it, I—"

"Shh." He stood upright again and used one crooked finger to reposition her head. "Let me finish this."

"You don't have to. I can take care of my own hair, I think. I've been taking care of it and myself for a very long time now."

"You've been taking care of everyone for a very long time, April. Maybe it's time you let someone else take care of you."

"Take care of me?"

"You know, for a while. A few days?"

He didn't say it like the offer of a man to a woman with whom he hoped to build a future or even have a fling with. He said it as if—as if he wanted her approval. Let me do this for a few days and it will…what? Assuage his guilt over the way he behaved? "I don't think this is wise, Kurt."

"A few minutes then? Let me do this for you now and we can take up where we left off again later."

"Where we left off?"

"*Animosity* is the word I believe you used."

"I remember."

His fingers worked gently over her scalp, freeing bits of leaves and sticks along the way and sending tingles down her spine.

He took a long, deep breath and held it, then let it out slowly. Then his fingers began to work again. He swept the brush downward again. "There. All done."

A lump rose in April's throat. She closed her eyes.

"Of course, you know…" He gathered her hair in one hand again and let it fall over her shoulder. His blunt, callused fingers grazed the now-exposed nape of her neck.

Her breath caught high in her chest.

He took a step back and said, "This is just, you know, not reality. Not *our* reality. It's just a few minutes of our lives sheltered from the world. But eventually, the world—Wileyville, our friends and families—will seep back in and all the demands and demons will be back. These few minutes won't change anything."

She nodded, then opened her mouth to speak, but he had already gone.

"It doesn't change a thing," she whispered. She shifted so she could watch him walking slowly toward the big old empty house with his head high, his dog bounding around his feet and the weight of the world seeming to rest on his broad, capable shoulders. "Except that it makes me wish more than ever that I knew what hurt you hope to hide from by coming out here so I could understand you. So I could finally forgive you."

Chapter Eight

He was digging his own grave. "And getting in deeper by the minute."

Kurt propped his foot on the edge of the spade and shoved the blade into the damp, dark ground.

Matilda woofed and settled down in the shade of the gray stone wall.

"I never should have been alone with April out here," he muttered. Even though his fingers ached from gripping the old garden tool, he could still feel how soft April's hair had felt wrapping around his knuckles. "And I already regret telling her that she could do anything she wanted to bring back the garden while she was out here."

But what could he do? She'd walked through his front door yesterday after their encounter, her hair unbound and her cheeks glowing from working in the sun all afternoon. And she had smiled at him, all shylike, the way she had the first day he saw her in the Weed 'Em and Reap shop.

He'd have given her anything that day. He did, in fact, give her his heart. Right there and then, in exchange for that singular perfect smile. Only he was wise enough not to have ever told her that.

And stupid enough not to have told her about the COCW thinking he'd taken her and Miss Cora on as his personal Lenten season project.

"I *ought* to be digging a grave," he grumbled, lifting another spade full of dirt. "Because when she finds that out, she's going to kill me."

A lot of people didn't realize it, but April Shelnutt had her pride. Not the puffed-up, foolish, blind-to-what-everybody-else-can-see-in-ten-seconds-about-you kind of pride that so many people mistook for—what did they call it these days?—self-esteem. No, April was the kind who understood that real esteem did not actually come through the self but from belonging to the Lord and finding ways to live like Him. But she did have this other side, this part of her that couldn't stand the perceived pity of others.

As for him? Pity, pride, amusement or scorn—what other people thought of him just didn't matter much at all. All he wanted at the end of the day was to be able to live with himself. He'd *have* to since he planned on living *by* himself until the end of his life.

So the question nagged at him. Could he live with himself if what he did caused others to look at April with the one thing by which she could not abide?

He threw the spade full of dirt over his shoulder, sending the scent of damp earth into the cool mid-March air. The clods and bits of rock landed a little too close to Matilda to suit her. She sneezed and gave him a disapproving look, then heaved herself up and went to lie in a sunny patch well out of hailing-dirt range.

"Sorry, girl. Guess I just have a way with females, huh?"

She plunked her body down, her back to him.

"A way of making them wish I'd fall off the face of the earth." Until now, April had seemed willing to share the planet with him, as long as each of them kept to his and her own turf, but when she found out what he'd let Sadie unleash to save his unmarrying hide…

"The way I see it—or *hear* it, straight from Sadie's lips—I had two choices. Go with April as a project or as the COCW's prime nice girl to run at me in hopes of inspiring the happily ever after, till-death-do-us-part thing."

Matilda sighed and shifted in the dried grass, already speckled with green and the promise of spring.

"But I am not going to walk down that infamous aisle ever again." Period. He'd made up his mind on that subject years ago. So what they—the well-intentioned matchmakers—would end up causing the female target of their marriage-minded meddling would be nothing short of a pointed, painful, public rejection. *No, I will not marry April Shelnutt.*

And then the speculation would start. Blame would be assigned. Fingers pointed. And it would be a very long time, if ever, before he or April could walk into Owtt's or the Not by Bread Alone Bakery or even church without the hushed words and furtive glances.

"What went wrong there?"

"Did he dump her or she him?"

"You know about his late wife, don't you?"

And Kurt's worst nightmare would begin again. Only this time, it would not just encompass his own shortcomings or the suppositions about his marriage and the woman who had died before she could make anyone understand why she did what she did. This time, the unstoppable rumor mill that was Wileyville would target April, too. And that would crush her.

He just could not let that happen.

No, opening his big mouth had already been the root of too much pain in his life. As it stood, Sadie was the one who'd put forth the idea of April and Miss Cora as Kurt's benevolence project, not him. He never said any such thing.

To the COCW, his taking on April as a project came with the built-in proviso that he would not put any moves on her. Romancing someone you had promised to help reeked of taking advantage, breaking the rules by which men of honor abide.

"So digging my own grave it is," he grumbled. "And when April finds out—and she will find out— at least, she'll have a nice place to hide the body."

There were worse things than leaving a woman with a world of righteous indignation at your rotten behavior, he justified. So he'd wait until the end and then drop it on her. That way she'd have reason to detest him. Everyone in Wileyville would support her in that sentiment. No one would pity her.

They'd rally around her, in fact. And probably stop speaking to him. "Bonus!"

Matilda jerked her head up.

"Don't mind me, girl. Just a little advance celebration for when April and Miss Cora go back to Wileyville and I move out here and life goes on just the way I imagined it." He pushed the blade into the soil at the bottom of the two-foot hollow he'd created. "Secluded."

He scooped up more dirt. "Solitary."

He tossed it over his shoulder. "Sad."

The metal tip pinged against a rock. "Existence."

He stared into the hole. "I can hardly wait."

Ignoring him completely, Matilda leapt to her feet at the sound of someone's approach.

Kurt barely had a chance to turn toward the gateway when a familiar voice bellowed "Hold up, badge boy!"

The dog made a dash for the pretty lady with the long, soft braid.

Despite the fact that he'd have liked to hurry off and greet her, too, Kurt planted the shovel tip in a grassy spot, leaned against the handle and waited for her.

"Those holes need to be wider with the soil really loosened up." Rolling a wagon filled with plants behind her, she pointed to his work space and shouted "We're planting lilacs there, not burying hazardous waste."

"You sure?" He swiped the hem of his T-shirt over his forehead. "Because I thought I heard Miss Cora say something about wanting to find a safe way to dispose of last night's meat loaf."

"Oh, yeah?" She peered at him over the broken-down garden wall, her eyes narrow and her mouth crooked in a tell-that-to-somebody-who'll-buy-it smile. "I noticed you had seconds of my special all-organic meat loaf at dinner *and* took some of it with you."

"Yeah, well, I've been needing a doorstop so—"

She jabbed her finger toward the ground and snarled happily. "Dig!"

"Yes, ma'am." He grinned but kept his head down and put his entire body to work to keep her from seeing how much her showing up had pleased him. Okay, that wasn't wholly true. He did duck to keep her from seeing his face, but the full-body flexing of his muscles just to get the ground ready for a lilac bush? *That* he did for her benefit alone. Yeah, Kurt

Muldoon, ex-army officer and current county sheriff, was showing off for a girl.

"Only don't get carried away," she called.

"Thanks for reminding me." He relaxed a bit and used the shovel's edge to scrape a dirt clod from his boot. "You bring the plants in, I'll take care of this part of it."

"Do you promise?"

He jerked his head up to find her gaze intently focused on him. "Promise?"

"To take care of this place after..." She made a halfhearted gesture toward the road that led away from Ezra's Holler and back to Wileyville. Her shoulders rose and fell. She scanned the plot they had finished clearing of dead growth yesterday and sighed. "Getting what little bit I can into the ground before Miss Cora is well enough to go home won't turn this back into a real garden by itself, you know."

"It'll be fine, I'm sure."

"I don't know. It's really a couple of weeks too early to be putting these in the ground."

"They'll be fine. Trust me."

To her credit, she did not throw all the reasons she had *not* to trust him in his face.

Of course, he thought, she didn't even *know* all the reasons.

Instead, she tugged her collar up against the stir of wind at her back and said, "It's been so mild this winter. It probably won't hurt to go ahead and get them in."

"Not unless we get a late freeze."

"Shh!" She turned and spoke directly to the small, bundled branches poking up over the top of the wall beside her. "Don't listen to him. Once spring comes to Kentucky, it sticks around."

"April, I've heard of talking to plants, but telling them untruths—"

"*Half* truths, maybe," she corrected him. "But I honestly do think spring is going to come early this year. In fact, I'm counting on it. And *you*."

Her eyes were fixed on his. He wanted to look away, but he had to ask "Me?"

"Yes, I'm counting on you to take care of all the saplings and bulbs and seedlings I'm trying to start growing here again."

He wanted to warn her to be more careful about what she counted on. Instead, he nodded, then looked toward the old fountain and said, "Whatever you set up out here, I'll do my best to keep alive. But I can't promise I'll be any good at it. I'm an old army man, April. Nurturing things was not in my training."

"Neither is restoring an old house or upkeep on the outbuildings."

"Outbuildings? Those need upkeep? I figured that ended when they installed indoor plumbing." He scratched the back of his head and played up the big ol' army oaf bit but good. "'Course I have dug my share of latrines, ma'am, so I guess—"

"Out*buildings*, not out*houses*. The church, the

school, the jail." She made careful quarter turns to face each structure she named before bringing her gaze to rest on him again, her expression one of genuine concern. "You don't just plan to let those sit uncared for and fall apart, do you?"

"Well, I can't rightly put them to their intended uses now, can I? I don't have credentials to teach or a congregation to preach to."

Her smile came slow and tentative. "Guess that just leaves you to do some private sheriffing in your spare time."

"You mean become a bounty hunter like that guy on TV?" Yes, he *did* flex his muscles. A bit. Just trying to give the bulked-up macho bit its due. "I'd have to let my hair grow out and get myself a real mean-sounding nickname."

"Kurt 'Digger' Muldoon? I don't think so." She crinkled up her nose. "Besides, you can't be a sheriff and a bounty hunter, too."

He jabbed the shovel into the earth, again and again. "Not like I plan to be a sheriff forever."

"But for a while longer, right?"

He lifted one last pile of loose dirt and dumped it onto the ground by his feet. "Okay, ready for planting."

"Kurt? You *are* going to run for sheriff again next term, aren't you?"

He hadn't told a single soul about his plans. He wouldn't have, but this was April, and she was asking outright. He let the shovel fall away and, as he swiped his hands together, lowered his chin and locked eyes with her. "I'm not even sure I'm going to stay in office for the rest of *this* term."

"You're..." She blinked. Shook her head. "You can't mean that."

"Why not?" He finished swiping the dirt from his palms and motioned to her to bring the plants to him. "Wileyville doesn't need me. I only ran because I hoped it would help me..."

She pulled the wobbly-wheeled red wagon over the roughed-out path and stopped beside the hole he just finished digging, waiting.

He reached his hands out to take one of the bare-limbed lilacs with its roots wrapped in coarse burlap.

"You thought it would help you what, Kurt? Somehow make up for something you had done wrong?"

"No." He did not tell a lie. He knew that nothing he could do or become could erase his past mistakes. "Look, I may not get to a real church all that often— and, believe me, I hear about it from my mother— but I get the concept of handing my sins over to Jesus, scarlet robes washed white again. I totally get that."

It was more than he had said about his spiritual walk to anyone since his wife died.

"I believe and rely on it, so don't go trying to read anything like that into my taking local office. I did

not do it as an act of penance or to try and counterbalance a lifetime of misdeeds."

She bent down and put her hands on the lilac's
trunk just above his. "I didn't know your misdeeds
stretched back over a whole lifetime."

"There's a lot you don't know about me, April."

"So I gather."

"You don't know why I ran for sheriff and you
wouldn't understand why I'm leaving."

"I could, Kurt. I'd like to, if you would just…"

What he just had to do was take charge. Always.
He worked his fingers into the twine that bound the
roots of the plant and tugged it from the wagon bed.
"So do I take the burlap off first or just put the whole
thing in the ground as is?"

She watched him in silence for a few seconds,
then bent down to take the plant from him. "I'll do
this. You should start digging another hole across the
way."

She shrugged one shoulder to direct his attention
to the spot on the other side of the garden entrance
where she wanted to place the other lilac.

He obliged her without another word, pressing the
tip of the spade into the ground with one sharp push.

He wanted to tell her everything. Of course, he
knew he could never do that. Maybe he did have
some pride, after all. Maybe he did care what people
thought of him—some people, at least.

He lifted some dirt up from the designated spot.

April patted some dirt down around the young lilac.

He wiped away a trickle of sweat from the back of his neck.

April got a bucket from the wagon and poured water around the new planting. They went on like that in silence until Dr. Joyce's car came up the driveway.

The woman hopped out, waved to them and hurried inside to see her patient.

"How's Miss Cora doing anyway?" he asked, not just to chase away the chilling quiet but to gauge how much longer he would have to stay away from his own home and put his planned future on the back burner.

His burden.

"Okay. Healing good, I think. But last night, she had a hard time breathing, and I worried that—"

"April! Sheriff!" Dr. Joyce strained to reach out over the porch railing to make herself be seen and heard. She waved her arms. She motioned for them to come. "Hurry!"

Kurt took off at full speed, his heart pounding. He didn't wait even a second for April. He couldn't. Someone needed him and he had to be there.

That was why he had become a sheriff, after all. To respond. To act. To help. To save lives if God put them in his power to do so. Without judgment or hesitation. He had shown both only one time before, and that had left him bitter, confused, angry and *widowed*.

"If Miss Cora is all right," he muttered under his breath, not quite a prayer, not quite a vow, "she and April can stay here as long as they like. Forever even. Just let her be all right. Just let me not be too late to help. Just let…"

He hit the steps, wrenched open the old screen door and thundered over the old wooden floors to the bedroom. What he found waiting for him stopped him dead in his tracks.

Chapter Nine

"What…? Why did you…?"

April pushed past Kurt and threw her arms open wide. "You're sitting! Miss Cora, you're sitting!"

The old woman smiled like a toothless tot who'd just taken her first steps. "Ta-da!"

"*Sitting?* That's why the doctor called for us to rush in here?" He gulped down some air as if he had to prove that the unjustified effort had left him winded.

April laughed and tried not to think about how adorable he looked trying to act all grumpy and put upon when only seconds ago he'd run at breakneck speed to offer his help. And he'd offered a prayer for Miss Cora's well-being, promising the only thing he kept telling everyone he did not want: to share his home forever, if the need arose. How could she stay mad at a guy like that?

Confirmed. April Shelnutt was a first-rate patsy. And that was just fine with her.

"I thought you'd be happy, Sheriff." Miss Cora pulled out all the stops, pouting, batting her eyelashes and twiddling with the ribbon on the high collar of her nightdress. "If I can sit here, I can sit in a car. And if I can sit in a car, I can get out of your hair." She gave a curt nod. "And your *house,* too!"

"Don't you feel you have to hurry yourself too fast for that, Miss Cora." April patted the proud woman's slightly hunched back, then fluffed and arranged the wisps of white hair on her head. "I have it on excellent authority that he's not going to throw us out until we're good and ready to be thrown."

"Authority?" Miss Cora's eyes grew wide. "Whose?"

"His." April straightened and folded her arms, all but daring Kurt to deny it.

He ducked his head, muttering, "Heard that, did ya?"

"Yes." She met his gaze and held it.

He smiled. Just a little. A kid-caught-with-his-hand-in-the-cookie-jar kind of smile, to be sure, but there all the same and just for her.

Maybe *patsy* was too strong a word for her and her inability to stay mad at the guy. Maybe she had simply turned a corner and unexpectedly found herself on the way to finally forgiving him. Whatever happened, that moment of potential crisis had given her just enough of a glimpse of the man beneath his strong, silent act that she just couldn't view him as selfish or manipulative anymore.

She had seen Kurt in that moment. *Really* seen him. Not the man he wanted to present others, but the man she had always known was within. A man who put others' needs ahead of his own desires. A man striving, first and foremost, to serve and help. A man of faith.

A man not too hard on the eyes in a work-worn T-shirt and faded jeans.

"I heard you," she said softly. "And I'm going to hold you to it."

"Good." Dr. Joyce blew by them both and began to gather the medical supplies she had laid out on the end table beside the wingback chair, where Miss Cora was seated. "Because as Miss Cora's doctor, I think she could use another full day or so of recuperation before she heads back to her new place."

"Really? You think so?" April had noticed that the older woman seemed thinner but hadn't mentioned it for fear that someone—okay, Kurt—would turn the fact into a joke about April's cooking. Then there was the trouble she'd had breathing last night. April studied Miss Cora's lined face. "Is—is something wrong?"

"Not with Miss Cora. No, nothing beyond needing to be a little more careful where she sticks her—" Cora cleared her throat "—nose. No more tree climbing for you, my dear."

The toothless grin flashed again.

The doctor narrowed one eye and wagged a finger of warning. "And watch that backside."

"If I was limber enough to *watch* that, I'd have been limber enough to get those dead bits off the dogwood before the window clamped down on me, Missy." Miss Cora sniffed indignantly.

"Good point." The doctor laughed, then raised her eyes to April. "Actually, it's a front that has me concerned."

Miss Cora scooted to the edge of the grand old wingback chair. "What's wrong with my front?"

"Not *your* front. *A* front." Dr. Joyce looked first to April, then to Kurt. "Cold front moving in. Heard on the radio driving in. They say to prepare for a change. Could drop as much as fifteen degrees below normal for this time of year."

"Fifteen degrees?" April might not know a lot about men in general, but she knew what weathermen meant when they talked about a cold front. "That could get near freezing."

"Ah, those duded-up TV people!" Miss Cora waved her hand. Her nose crinkled. "They don't know God's business."

"How's this place heated?" April looked around for heat registers on the floor first, then along the wall.

"Propane." Kurt wagged his head toward what April could guess was the direction of the large outside tank. "But the house has sat empty all winter. I don't think we can use it."

"Yeah, I have propane myself," the doctor said. "You shouldn't just turn on the heating system without an inspection first."

"Who needs a fancy heating system? We have perfectly good fireplaces and plenty of blankets."

April looked at Kurt.

"Have to side with Miss Cora on this one," he said.

"Of course!" The old gal beamed.

"The weathermen don't know God's business," he repeated, grinning. "I can't tell you how many times since I took office that some weather report got people all stirred up. And much as I admire most folks in town, they do tend to start calling the switchboard at the sign of the first flake."

"Not to mention cleaning out the stores of bread, milk and eggs." The doctor finished collecting her things. "Speaking of which, I better get going into town to get my share before the shelves are bare. Can I bring y'all out anything?"

"No! Please don't. The COCW sends tons of food out with Kurt every time he comes. In fact, if the grocery store is picked over, stop by here and take what you want. We can't possibly eat it all in the next day or so."

Kurt laced his arms over his chest and lifted his chin. "Don't be so sure."

April gripped the back of Miss Cora's chair. "Why?"

"Well, it sounds like not only do I have to finish

up in the garden now but I better chop some wood for the fireplace, too."

"My hero." April clasped her hands to her cheek and cooed.

"Just doing my duty for the womenfolk, ma'am." He tugged at the band of his jeans and puffed up his chest, teasing, "All that manly work can make a fellow pretty hungry."

"Hungry enough to eat *my* cooking?"

"Hmm, you have a point." He took a step toward April and leaned down to ask in an almost-intimate tone, "Shall we ask the doctor to stick around in case we need assistance after dinner?"

"Don't bother, I'm out of here." And she was, out the door and gone, calling out, "Give me a ring when you're ready to transport Miss Cora back to Wileyville!"

"She sure was in a hurry," Kurt grumbled.

"You think it was talk about my cooking?"

"I think it was mentioning how goofy people act when they hear it's going to snow." His eyebrows lowered and he frowned. "Probably made her anxious to get back to the office."

April nodded as she studied Kurt's stormy expression. "How about you?"

His lips lifted into a smile, but not much of one. "I never act goofy, snow or no snow."

"No, do you have to get back to the office?"

"You're just trying to get out of cooking me

dinner, aren't you?" The smile came full on now and it warmed April in ways no fancy propane heating, as Miss Cora might say, ever could.

"I'm only thinking of you and your poor stomach." She was flirting. A little. Harmlessly, of course, with Miss Cora right there in the chair in front of her. "Oh, and the people of Wileyville who may need you to come to their rescue."

"I have a radio in my truck and a cellphone in my pocket. If the people of Wileyville need me, they can get me."

"Lucky them." Did she *say* that? She knew she'd thought it, but had she actually spoken the words aloud?

Kurt glanced away. He rubbed the back of his neck and shifted his weight, anything to avoid looking at April and acknowledging the unvarnished wistfulness of her whispered remark.

At last, he cleared his throat and clapped his hands together, hard. "Guess I'll go back to the garden and finish up, then hit that woodpile."

"I have a better idea." Suddenly, April wanted out of the room and out of the house that would only remind her of everything she would never have. Besides, the pent-up energy that resulted from her latest unguarded moment necessitated a workout. "*I'll* chop the wood and you cook."

Halfway to the door, he twisted his head to catch her eye over his shoulder. "You don't think I can, do you?"

"Can what?" she ventured from behind Miss Cora's chair. "Cook or let a woman chop wood in your place?"

"Either."

"No, I don't think you can do either," she said, her head angled high.

"Okay, you're on then." He pointed to her and winked. "I'll finish in the garden, then report for duty in the kitchen."

He pivoted to leave.

"Okay." She gave a curt nod. "I'll chop the wood, get the fireplaces ready, get cleaned up and meet you down here in time to set the table."

Off April started.

As she pressed past Kurt in the hallway, from the bedroom came the prim-and-proper-and-just-a-wee-bit-peeved voice of Miss Cora. "I guess I'll just sit here!"

April tended to Cora and got the wood chopped and the fire started.

Kurt planted the lilacs, got cleaned up and had dinner waiting in the dining room when April entered with her hair still damp from taking a shower.

"Where's Miss Cora?" she asked, bunching the quilt that she had found upstairs around her shoulders to ward off the chill in the drafty old house.

Kurt held a lit match to the wick of the last of five tapers in the silver candelabra. "Once she got settled in on the couch next to that blazing fire you built, I couldn't get her to budge."

"Should we fix a tray of food and take it—"

"Not necessary." He shook the match to put out the flame, then stood back, his face lit up as much with pride as from the glow of the mismatched candles. "Miss Cora wandered in while I was cooking and insisted I immediately reheat some of the casserole that Claudia Addams sent out for her."

"Bossy little thing, ain't she?" April laughed and took the chair Kurt pulled out for her at one end of the table.

"And impatient to boot. She let me know that she thought expecting her to wait until almost seven for her supper was my way of trying to give her stomach troubles."

"I've really enjoyed looking after her these last few days."

He nodded, pulled the chair out nearest her on the side of the table and sat down.

"Aren't you going to take the head of the table?" When he had stayed to share a meal the night before, they had eaten at the kitchen table, Kurt and she at the ends, Miss Cora in the middle and Matilda watching from a mat across the room.

Kurt craned his neck as if he couldn't quite make out the chair all the way at the end of the long, polished table, then turned to her and offered his hand. "If I did that, how could we pray together?"

She pulled up her shoulders and dropped her hands to her lap. "We don't have to hold hands to pray together, Kurt."

He did not budge an inch. "Food is getting cold, April."

She studied his rugged palm, the long fingers, the pinkish spots here and there where tomorrow there would be new blisters from using the spade. No, not from the spade. His hands had calluses in all the right places to protect against blisters. Grabbing a pan from the oven without a mitt. That had to be it.

Too bad she hadn't been in the kitchen to…

To what? Lighten his workload so he wouldn't have made a hasty mistake? Rush in and save him from himself at the very last moment? Kiss it and make it better?

Something fluttered in the pit of her stomach.

"April?" He edged his hand closer to her. "Shall we bless the food?"

Deep breath. "Yes."

She slid her hand in his and shut her eyes.

"Dear Father," he began, low and reverent. "Thank You for this day, this place, this food. Thank You for the blessing of serving You by helping others. Thank You for the honor of being served by those who only want to do what's right, even if what they do and what we think they should do aren't the same thing. In Jesus' name. Amen."

"Amen." She shook out the cloth napkin and lay

it in her lap. *Let the small talk begin!* "Nice of you to remember the COCW in your blessing."

"Did I?"

"People who want to do what's right, even if we don't… You did mean the COCW, didn't you?"

"Sweet potatoes?" He swung the bowl of buttered orange slices under her nose. "Miss Cora said they were almost as good as the ones she used to make herself."

What had she thought? That Sheriff McSecrecy would suddenly burst forth with the underlying meaning of…*anything?* Not that that was going to keep her from trying to get something out of the man. She heaped sweet potatoes onto her plate and topped the side dish with a helping of persistent curiosity. "You and Miss Cora find much to talk about over her early dinner?"

"This and that." He served himself.

Me? she wanted to ask. Miss Cora had never held back her opinion when it came to April and Kurt, whether it was to point out that they looked powerfully cute together or because she thought each of them harbored some kind of pain that kept April and Kurt from either moving forward with a relationship or moving on without one. "So she didn't, uh, talk to you about, oh, dead limbs? Encouraging things to bloom?"

Mouth full, he shook his head. When he'd swallowed and swiped the napkin over his lips, he asked,

"Why, did she talk to you about some chores she thinks I should tackle?"

"You might say that." April stabbed at the food on her plate with the tines of her fork. "But it's the kind of thing she'd have to tell you herself."

"If she remembers it."

"Hmm." She feigned intense interest in her biscuit.

"Funny thing. She forgets things we tell her from day to day, but she recalls every detail of growing up and living out here. As far back as eighty years ago, she can tell you what it was like down to every sight, smell and sound. Then she looks right at you and asks who you are and why you haven't done whatever she had in mind that you should have done for her yet."

"I know, I know."

The aromas of the odd collection of dishes— mostly leftovers courtesy of the meals sent out by the ladies of the COCW—filled the room. But it was no substitute for the sound of Kurt's voice.

"So what did Miss Cora tell you then about living out here?"

"Talked about the house, about how her father brought in craftsmen from Virginia to do the staircase and carved-wood pieces. How they put the school up in a single afternoon with the help of people who'd come out here to live. And how they saved the money he made as an itinerant preacher to build the church."

"And the jail?"

"The jail came later."

"I guess he hoped his new town wouldn't need one."

"To hear Miss Cora tell it, if he'd had his way, he'd have constructed that first."

"Oh?"

"Have to hand it to her, she didn't pull any punches. Went on and on about how her daddy's biggest downfall was his inability to deal with his *own* sins."

She put her elbows on the table and leaned in.

"Made a real point of letting me know that the esteemed Ezra Barrett tried to found an entire town, to create a place to hide from his own demons. That, because he had not always practiced the art of self-discipline, he decided to come here, where discipline would be imposed by the very nature of the place."

She smiled. "Miss Cora and the liniment sales-man."

"What?"

"I was thinking about what she told me it took to grow up out here. It couldn't have been easy, and you sure couldn't have survived without *some* kind of discipline. But without self-discipline? Seems old Ezra was foolin' himself if he thought the ready-made restraints of work and survival could replace that."

"I suppose." He dove into his meal again.

She watched the candlelight play over his hair. Funny, she had never noticed the gray before. Or that this man, for all his bravery on the job past and present, could not look her in the eye. Her words had hit a nerve with him.

"Appears Miss Cora figured out what her daddy missed, though."

"Hmm."

"And shared it with you because…" She let the thought trail off to try to pull him into the conversation.

He set his fork aside, pushed his chair back and met her gaze. "You think you know why I've come out here, April? Is that what you're implying? That you've got it figured out that Miss Cora was trying to warn me about coming out here to hide from myself? That I won't be any better at it than her father was?"

She tried to swallow. Suddenly, the heat from the candles made her cheeks burn. "Well, I—"

"Okay. Maybe you're right. And maybe Miss Cora is right. And maybe her father and I, we have it all wrong. But right or wrong, it's *my* choice. My business why I want to come out here." He threw his napkin down by his plate. "And by the way, your opinion might hold a little more weight if you had told me why *you* came here. Why you *really* came."

"I told you, I came here to forgive you." She chose not to remind him that he thought she'd come here to get over him. "That's the truth."

"I just don't get it."

"Why I can't forgive what you did?"

"Why you'd even want to," he whispered.

"To break away the dead limbs," she said softly. *So I can bloom.*

She saw it now. The pain he carried, though over what she couldn't guess. Her? No, something beyond her. Something that had made him treat her the way he did, perhaps.

"April, I—" he shook his head "—I'm sorry."

"For what?" She wanted to hear him say it. She needed that.

"For, well, for everything, I guess." He rubbed his hand back through his hair. "I know it's not enough, not nearly enough, but…"

She put her hand on his raised wrist. "Then give me more."

He eased his arm down and away from her touch. "More?"

"Tell me more. Tell me…anything, Kurt. Besides 'I'm just a very private guy,' 'I don't want everybody in town knowing my business.' Tell me the *why* behind what I already know."

"It wouldn't change anything, April. It won't change how I feel."

"It might change how *I* feel."

"How *do* you feel?"

"Like I have on the full armor of God. Only I have it on for all the wrong reasons—to keep people out instead of to protect against evil."

"I don't follow."

"When Hannah, Sadie and I were little, Daddy gave us each a Bible verse that he would shorten into a phrase to remind us of his expectations for us. Sadie's was 'Wait on the Lord.'"

"Sadie? Your sister Sadie? The one who rushes headlong into everything?"

"That's the one." April often marveled at how the verses had been pinpoint accurate about the girls' personalities. If ever a person needed to be told to wait, it was Sadie. And then there was high-strung Hannah. "'Peace. Be still.' That was for my youngest sister, Hannah."

"Hannah? Who moved to Ohio and wrote those crazy columns for the local paper about how hectic her life was all the time?"

April nodded and laughed. "If it helps, they both found new verses for the next stages of their lives. But me…"

"You?"

"'Gird your loins.'" She sighed. "That's what Daddy used to say to remind me not to let my guard down. I know he meant spiritually. I know he worried that, since I was only his stepchild, one day someone might come along and take me away, so he wanted to know I would always be protected by God's love and, no matter what, I'd stand. But…"

"But it was a lot to bear for a kid who also had to keep the secret of how sick her mother had been."

"I thought I'd finally broken free of all that."

"Then I came along and put demands on you to keep our love a secret or—"

"Love?"

"Hmm?"

"You never called it *love* before."

"And I shouldn't have now. It doesn't change anything."

"Are you kidding? Love changes everything, Kurt."

"Does it help you forgive me so that you can move on? Because my choices are not based on my feelings, April. They are based on my beliefs. They are based on my experiences. They are based on my reality. And while it would be great if that included love and a relationship, it has to be in a way that works for me. That's nothing less than you want for yourself. We just want different things, April, and that's all there is to it." The legs of his chair scooted across the floorboards, followed by the sound of his footsteps out in the hallway heading to the front door. "I'm going to get some fresh air before I clean up these dishes and go home."

"Kurt?" She jumped up and hurried after him. "Why does that have to be all there is to it? Why can't we work together to find something that works for both of us?"

Of course, she knew the answer even before she asked the question. The hurt he carried inside—*that* he would not even talk about. April had exposed hers, told him everything, but what had he shared with her?

Keep our love a secret.

Love. That was what he had shared, and April could not watch him walk out that door.

"Whoa!" She yanked the door open and swept through the screen door in one fell swoop. More falling than swooping as her feet hit the slippery porch floor and sent her sprawling.

"I've got you." Kurt caught her under the arms and pulled her upright and right up into his arms.

She clutched at his shoulders.

"Careful," he said softly, his face so close, she could see several white crystals that had blown onto his eyelashes.

"It's snowing," she whispered. She pressed her palms flat against his chest to steady herself and found her footing.

"I know." He slid his arm down to circle her waist, less supporting her and more holding her close. "You okay?"

That depended on his definition of *okay,* she thought, her pulse pounding through her entire body, heat rising in her cheeks, weakness settling in her knees.

"April?" His eyes searched hers.

"It's just…" She wet her lips. *Love?*

The words he'd spoken moments earlier rang in

her ears. *My choices are not based on my feelings, April. They are based on my beliefs. They are based on my experiences. They are based on my reality.*

Big, fat, sloppy flakes plopped onto the walkway and stuck in the budding bushes just beyond the porch.

"Dogwood winter," she finished, pushing away from him at last.

"Huh?"

"A cold snap after the dogwoods have begun to bloom. They used to call it a dogwood winter." That was how she would forever think of this night between them. The cold that came after love had begun to bloom. "Not a killing frost but harsh enough to alter the bud, to take the color out of the blossom for a season or—"

He gave her no warning. Just pulled her close and placed his lips on hers. Passion? She did not think of it in terms of passion. She thought of it in terms of…healing.

Perhaps this was not a dogwood winter in their relationship but actually the first sign of something new beginning to grow. She wound her arms around his neck and kissed him back, her eyes closed and her heart filling with hope that, somehow from this point on, all would be well.

"Girl! Where's that girl? Is Lollie's boy around? I can't…I need help…"

Chapter Ten

"Reckon it's some kind of testimony to my faith that I find waking up here still on this earthly plane a bit of a disappointment," Miss Cora said weakly from beneath the clear plastic oxygen mask. She only ventured to open one eye.

"Well, it's not a disappointment to me, if you don't mind my saying so." April hovered over the raised emergency-room bed. "You gave us quite a scare there, Miss Cora."

Both eyes open now, the white-haired woman squinted hard enough to send ripples of wrinkles above her cheeks and between her eyebrows. "Now why is that, young lady?"

"Seeing you there like that, fallen on the floor and hardly breathing." April smoothed her hand over the crisp bedding. "All I could think was—"

"There's a woman whose work is done," the

strained voice concluded. Frail, age-spotted hands reached out.

April took both of them in hers. "What?"

"That's what you should have thought." Cora shifted, uneasy in the snarl of tubes and wires attached to machines and monitors beside the bed. She coughed, slightly patted April's fingers and conjured up a sweet, serene smile as she pressed on to speak. "Cora Mae Barrett did her best. It didn't always work out the way she wanted, but she loved the Lord through it all, unceasingly."

"I know all that," April murmured. "Everyone does."

"Now He's calling her home and she is ready. No tears. No fears. No regrets."

Lovely as it all sounded, it made April sad to hear. She bowed her head, not wanting to show her own tears, fears and regrets to the brave, faithful servant of God. "Oh, Miss Cora."

"And then you know what I'd've hoped you'd think next?"

She shook her head, unable to meet the woman's gaze.

"I would've hoped you'd think, And here I am, just like her. If it were me lying on the floor breathing my last, I'd be ready."

April sniffled. The steady beating of her heart muffled the beeps and bleeps and blips and hissing of all the high-tech equipment around them. Under any other circumstances, she'd have gotten all riled up, or, at least, huffed out a sharp-edged chuckle at hearing herself compared with the town's oldest old maid. How many times had she fought against seeing herself lumped in with Miss Cora in that insulting stereotype? And here was the woman herself making that comparison, and April had to admit, she found herself seriously wanting. In this area, she was no match for the formidable old gal.

Ready for her own death? She wasn't even ready for Miss Cora's. Even though her mother had been dead for twenty years, April hadn't been prepared when she'd learned of it not all that long ago.

"If it were you lying here instead of me, girl, would you be ready?"

"No." April spoke frankly, then rushed to add "And not because I haven't accepted Christ or don't understand the gift of salvation. I wouldn't be ready to die, Miss Cora, because…"

Could she really say this out loud?

She glanced at the kind eyes following even the tiniest nuance in her face.

If she couldn't tell the one person in Wileyville who would understand—on her probable deathbed, no less—then April would live the rest of her life bearing alone the one secret that she had never shared.

"I'm not ready to die, Miss Cora, because I don't think I've ever really lived. Not the life I always longed for," she said softly.

"You know, being married is not the only way to be really alive, of course?" Miss Cora smiled.

"No, it has nothing to do with whether or not I ever get married. You know that, Miss Cora. I'd like to be married. I want to be loved and cherished by someone like…" April studied the faded painting of a lone tree in a summer meadow on the far wall. "But I know that's not the only measure of a woman's life."

"Good."

"I just wish…I wanted…I've spent all my life doing exactly what I thought everybody else wanted. What everybody else needed me to do for them to get the things they wanted most in life. For Daddy, to hold the family together. For my sisters, to be the one who protected our past so they could move forward and have marriages and families and careers. For Kurt, to keep quiet about our feelings so that he could… That's the worst. I don't even know why he did it. The others, you know, at least I knew why. Him? It just seemed he was all too ready to use my vulnerability for his own convenience. Can you understand what I—"

The woman's sudden wracking cough cut off her thought.

April rose halfway up from her seat and glanced back through the glass door to see if a nurse was nearby to help.

The hall was empty.

"Shh." She checked the monitors—as if she would know what any of the flashing numbers meant—then ran her hand over Miss Cora's pain-creased forehead.

"I…" Another cough.

"Don't speak, Miss Cora."

"But I have to know…" A shuddering breath. A red-faced struggle to draw in air. "…about *you*, girl."

Tears washed over April's eyes. She set her chin, determined not to let emotion overwhelm her. "Don't worry about me."

"But I do," Cora rasped. She reached out to touch April's face. "You're the girl who's going to bring me my prize tomatoes. How can I not worry? When I leave you, you'll forget…"

"I won't forget you. Not ever, Miss Cora. Or your tomatoes," April whispered. She could envision just where she would put them in the garden. See the vines striving upward. Taste the sun-warmed burst of flavor on her tongue. "You'll see. I'll get them in soon and, come early September, you'll have the first slice."

"You can't predict that, girl." The tubing rustled with the shake of her head. "You don't know God's business."

"I know I'm not ready for you to go. I want to share those tomatoes with you. I want to share another growing season."

A feeble cackle answered her. "I think I've done

all the growing I'm going to do, child. Harvesttime has come."

April wanted to cover her ears and hide from the woman's candor. But she promised herself that her days of hiding were over. Her days of taking action had begun.

April searched the tangle of cords hanging limply all around the bed, found the one with the bright red button on it and pressed it, hard, once. And then again. And again.

It wasn't until the third time that she realized she was sobbing.

"Now don't you grieve." More coughing, quieter this time, but no less demanding on the tired little body. "It comes for all of us in time. God does his work on us, just like he does on those lilies of the field, and then…"

April pressed her lips together. Again, she looked around for help. No one.

Dr. Joyce had told them not to take her patient to the local hospital but to transport her to the larger facility two towns over. She said she'd be in as soon as she could.

Kurt had wanted to come, but with the late snow causing fender benders on the dark, winding country roads, he had to stay in county. April wished he was here.

"It wouldn't change anything," he'd probably tell her.

But it would.

She knew it would.

Love changed everything.

Kurt loved her. It might not mean that they would be able to make a life together, but just knowing it filled her heart with hope and joy. With love, anything was possible, right?

Buoyed by that thought, April stood. "Miss Cora, I'm going to step into the hall and insist that someone come in here to help you."

"No!" A gnarled hand shot out.

April froze.

"No. Now they gave me something for the discomfort. Said it would take hold soon and that Dr. Joyce is on her way. Nothing more they can do right now, girl." Another cough, this time ending in a wheeze and an outstretched hand. "There are other folks here who need the care more than me. Come sit with me."

April went to her, wiped the spittle from around her thin, pale lips, then brushed back a puff of frizzled white hair from the blue-veined temple. "All right. But don't talk, okay? Conserve your energy."

"Don't tell me what to do." Cora's throat sounded scratchy and rough. She fiddled around with the things on her nightstand and pulled out a tissue to hand to April. "Wipe your nose."

"Yes, ma'am."

"And tell me something." She managed to pull

herself a little more upright in the bed and patted a vacant place among the confusion of connecting cords and tubes and wires.

"What?" April said gingerly.

"I have always believed that God left me here on this earth long after everybody who ever knew me as a child or young woman had gone on to Him because He had His reasons." Her voice gained some of its familiar timbre.

"Teaching at the home." April said the first thing that came to mind. "You told me the day you asked me to take you out to Ezra's Holler that you were doing the Lord's work with that and planned to go right on doing it for another twenty years."

"Well, I may have miscalculated a bit on how long the Lord would need me in that line of service." She laughed, just barely. "But I do have this conviction, this feeling heavy on my heart, that there is one more thing I have yet to do."

"More teaching?"

"Always." She tried to hold a cough back and winced, then continued. "As long as there is someone who still has something to learn."

"If you still have a lesson for me—"

"I think you have a lesson for yourself," Cora said softly. "If I could tell it to you, I surely would. But this one? Girl, this one you have to learn on your own. Nobody else can help you except for me to remind you."

"Remind me?"

"That you're forgiven."

"I'm—I know, Miss Cora."

"Then isn't it time you started acting like it?"

"I do." *April? The perpetual good girl? The woman who never forgot that she must wear the full armor of God? The world's biggest patsy?* How could anyone accuse her of not acting as if she understood the most basic tenet of her faith? "At least, I think I do."

"Oh? Then why haven't you bloomed?"

One quick check to make sure she hadn't sat on an air hose and cut off vital oxygen to Miss Cora's brain. "What exactly are you talking about?"

"You. We had this discussion about you and Lollie's boy, remember?"

"About us being powerfully cute together?"

"No, not that one—though you are."

"About you thinking he liked me?"

"No, but he does."

He did. He *loved* her.

Not that that changes anything, his voice resounded in her head.

"No, about you both having a hurt inside you that's like a dead limb keeping you from growing."

"We never, that is, *Kurt* is the one with the hurt inside. I used to be that way, but then I realized I had to stop keeping everyone's secrets and I'm fine now."

"Decided you're no longer going to do the things

you shouldn't ought to have been doing in the first place is not the same thing."

"The same thing as what?"

"Forgiveness."

The solitary word that she kept coming back to hung in the room between them.

April touched her hair, which she had not braided for her dinner with Kurt. She placed her cool fingers at the base of her throat. She watched Cora fight to take in a shallow breath and, without thinking much about why she did it, drew in a deep breath of her own and held it.

"Are you talking about me not forgiving Kurt and all the other people who have wronged me? Not *really* forgiving them?" April looked at the painting again, willing herself to bring up any unresolved feelings for her sisters, her father or even Kurt. None came, and so she said, "Because I've done that, I think. I feel like I've finally done that."

"You can't have, young lady. Not until you've cut off the dead limb. Not until you've done the painful job of forgiving yourself."

"*Myself?* For what?"

"For not blooming, dear."

"For not living the wonderful life God made me for," April murmured, and even as the words left her lips, she felt them take root in her heart.

"We have to forgive ourselves, and then we have to forgive the people who hurt us. Because forgiveness is not about other people—it's about allowing God to work in us." Miss Cora's small body shuddered with her next breath, but her color had come back and her eyes still shone bright and fearless. "Forgiveness is God's way of preparing us to grow in Him, just like plowing and pruning are our ways of preparing the ground for plants to grow again."

"Oh, Miss Cora, nobody else ever put it like that to me." The old woman really was still here because she hadn't finished serving the Lord. What a remarkable person. What a joy to know. Suddenly, April couldn't help feeling ashamed at not wanting people to compare the two of them. If she could live the rest of her life with the kind of exuberance and thirst for the Lord that Miss Cora still had in her waning time on earth, she would never again have to wonder if she had truly lived.

"God has forgiven you, girl." The woman gave April's hand a squeeze, or as much of a squeeze as she could manage. "Isn't it time you put your heart in agreement with His plan?"

"Yes, ma'am," she whispered, her heart full and her mind swimming.

"Now you go out there and see what's keeping my doctor."

April leaned in to place a kiss on her soft, cool cheek. "Yes, ma'am."

"And remember…" Miss Cora put her hand alongside April's face to keep her close enough to hear the faint words "Forgiveness is not a feeling. Forgiveness is an action. So take action, girl, and go out and bloom."

Another kiss good-bye, just in case, then April kept her eyes on the old woman until she stepped through the glass door, caught her foot and went tumbling backward straight into—

"Someday you're going to trip coming out a door and I won't be there to catch you." Kurt steadied her on her feet much as he had on the porch at Ezra's Holler. Except this time, neither his touch nor his gaze lingered. "You okay?"

"Fine." She swept her hand down the dress she had worn for their dinner together. She'd chosen it because she thought the flattering cut and sheer colors had made her look somehow earthy and ethereal all at the same time. Suddenly, in the garish light of the sterile hallway, she wanted to wad it up in both hands and scream "Why didn't someone tell me this thing looks like I made it out of a shower-curtain left over from the 1980s?" Instead, she angled her chin upward and met Kurt's eyes with a tight smile. "How long have you been out here?"

"Long enough to watch you tending to Miss Cora in there. She's lucky you've been around to look after her."

"I don't believe in luck," April said firmly. "God puts us where He needs us, and if we leave ourselves open to serve Him, then those things just look lucky to people who don't see the big picture."

"You don't think I see the big picture, April?"

She hadn't really thought about that much until just now. "I don't think any of us sees the big picture, Kurt. What does it say in the Bible? We see 'through a glass, darkly?' Just shadows, just bits and pieces that we try to fit together and make our own sense of along the way."

She'd certainly done as much with him. Thought she'd discovered his motives, his misconduct, his mean streak. But she had just been looking at what Miss Cora might call the dead limbs. April didn't know what hurt this man carried inside. And unless he chose to reveal it all to her, she could only recognize that it existed and forgive him.

And with him standing here, so close she could hear his breathing and see how his pupils had grown huge in the bright light, it was easy to do. He was only a man, after all. Not the answer to her every hope and dream. A guy. A child of God, full of faults and foibles. Just like her.

She took a step back from him and mustered up a smile. "Guess things quieted down enough in Wileyville and thereabouts so you could get away?"

"Yeah. I decided it was safe to take the time to bring Dr. Joyce over. My truck does better on the ice than her car."

"Ice?"

"Just patches here and there, and with it dark, that makes for some tricky driving."

"It's still dark?" She had lost all sense of time in the windowless maze of rooms and curtains.

"After midnight. But Dr. Joyce says hat shouldn't keep us from taking Miss Cora home."

"Home?" Lost all sense of time and all sense of reality, it would seem. "What do you mean?"

"To *the* home, not back out to Ezra's Holler."

"Miss Cora thinks she's going to another home— her eternal one."

"She told you that?"

"Sort of."

"Well, according to Dr. Joyce, Miss Cora went through this same kind of thing every year around this time when she lived at Ezra's Holler. Even as a little kid. It's allergies."

"So all the while, she let me think she was on the verge of…" *That little pill.* "And I never even questioned it." *The pill and the patsy. What a great team they made!* "Harvesttime! Can you believe I fell for that?"

"Harvesttime? I don't get it."

"She turned our conversation into talk about her not seeing another growing season and the like just so she could use the time to teach me a lesson."

He laughed and motioned toward the reception area. "And that surprised you? How?"

She shot him a look but followed along. She had

a few things to tell this man and she wouldn't mind getting herself and her awful choice in dresses out of the glaring fluorescent light to do it.

He paused by the door to a room filled with vinyl-cushioned chairs, lit only by the picture on a muted TV. "So this charade Miss Cora played to teach you something, did it work?"

She peered inside to check for occupants. "I believe it did."

"What did you learn?" He motioned for her to go inside.

She remained in the doorway and turned to face him. "I learned that it's pruning time."

"She taught you about gardening?"

She touched his sleeve and rubbed the supple fabric between her thumb and forefinger. "She taught me about life."

He gave her a crooked smile. "By pretending to be dying?"

"She didn't pretend so much as let me use my imagination to make the leap to that conclusion."

He leaned in as if he wanted to impart a secret. "I've heard you Shelnutts are famous conclusion leapers."

"Yeah?" She fought the shiver that his nearness inspired and lifted her head. It put her face just inches from his. So close that, even in the dim light, she could see his eyes searching hers. But she did not back down. *Pruning time. Time to take action.* "Have you ever considered that sometimes we don't so much leap as we are pushed to those conclusions? And sometimes by the very people we thought we could trust to have our backs?"

"What are you looking for here, April? A confession? An apology? I've done both of those as best I could and it hasn't made—"

"An action." She raised her head again, closer still, and did not retreat physically, emotionally or spiritually.

His eyebrows angled down. He didn't seem to shake his head, but he must have because a lock of brown hair fell forward to brush the bridge of his nose. "Huh?"

"I'm through reacting to what happens to me, and I'm ready to get rid of the deadwood in my life and take action. And do you know one of the things I am going to do first?"

"Yeah?" he asked quietly.

"Forgive you."

"For what?" Quieter still.

She pressed her lips together, gathered her strength and broke off the metaphorical limb that she'd hung on to for far too long. "For everything you've done to me."

He looked away but only for a moment. He cleared his throat. He tucked his hands into the pockets of his faded jeans. When he met her gaze again, the lock of hair still across his brow, he stretched out his hand and brushed his knuckle lightly along her jaw. "Oh, April."

"What, Kurt?" she managed to whisper.

He dropped his hand, his eyes no longer locked with hers, as he let out a long breath and told her, "Maybe you should hold off on that, uh, *action*, until you *know* everything I've done."

Chapter Eleven

❦

"A project?"

Kurt had expected anger at the disclosure. Hatred even. But not the devastation he saw in April's eyes. It cut through him. And yet, he would not take back a single word he had said. She had to know. He had to tell her. And if that meant she never forgave him, well, maybe that would be the best for both of them.

"You told everyone that you've been going to Ezra's Holler all week because you'd taken on the care and feeding of the town's poor spinster ladies as your personal *project?*" She all but choked on the words.

"I didn't tell them that. It was…" No, he was not a man to point fingers. Sadie and even his own sister, Pat, might have goaded him into this ruse, but in the end, it had been his choice to go along with it. His responsibility to bear the fallout. "It doesn't matter how they got the idea. That's what I let them think."

"You? Who asked me to slink around in secrecy?" She did not raise her voice.

He wished she had.

It was the stillness of her response that got to him. Made him want to take her in his arms, kiss her temple and find a way to make her understand that he had done it because he *had* to. He tried to push her away, to close her out, to withdraw from her life emotionally and physically, but it had not been enough.

Because she loved him.

And he loved her.

And that wasn't ever going to lead to anything but heartache.

"You, who expected me to put your obsessive demand for privacy above everything? You held me up for public ridicule to save your own what, Kurt? What are you protecting?"

"You." He clenched his jaw and tried to hold her tear-washed gaze. "I thought I was protecting you."

Her shoulders sank. Her lower lip trembled, but her eyes stayed trained on his face. "Don't give me that."

"It's true," he whispered.

"You may well believe it's true," she said. At last, she broke eye contact, turning her upper body toward the empty waiting room. She leaned against the side of the door. The television flickered blue-and-gray light over her features as she spoke. "You may have done a first-rate job convincing yourself that's true, but that doesn't make it so. The truth is, you are protecting yourself, first and foremost."

"You'll get no argument from me." It wasn't an admission. It wasn't a denial.

She rolled her head to one side as if that might loosen the tension in her neck and shut her eyes. "Miss Cora says you're protecting yourself from a hurt you've been carrying inside. It's something you can't forgive yourself for and so you can't move past it."

"Miss Cora?" He stepped through the doorway, turning to stand in front of her. He bent at the knees to place his face in front of hers. He took her upper arms in his hands. He wanted to make sure that she heard him, that she heard herself. "You talked to Miss Cora about me? About my pain? My personal, private pain?"

"We weren't gossiping about you, Kurt." She spoke earnestly, not a shred of defensiveness in her tone or posture. "We just... We care about you, both of us. If there was anything I could do for you—"

"You could not make me the subject of speculation, that's what you could do." He kept his tone calm and even. He wasn't hurt or angry. He only wanted to make a point so there would be no mistake. Then he could extricate himself from this situation once and for all and leave. To go home and lick his wounds, he supposed April would think. And she'd be right. And it would be none of her business. "You can spare me acting all indignant because *I* allowed some women to think what they were going to think anyway."

"What they were going to think anyway?" She cocked her head. Her hair fell against her cheek. She pushed away from the door frame and stepped into the waiting room. He could not see her face, but he did not have to to know his words had hit their mark. "Why? Because the only thing I could possibly ever be to a man like you is an object of pity?"

"Did I *say* pity?" He hadn't. But then he'd known that was right where her own insecurities would lead her, hadn't he?

"Well, I think you've got that backwards, Kurt." She moved into the light spilling into the darkened room from the hallway. Her beautiful eyes were all flash and fire, her cheeks flushed. Her whole body practically trembled but not in a way that made her seem meek. "You're the one who should be pitied."

"You're probably right," he said quietly. So quietly, she didn't seem to hear him at all.

"At least, I finally figured out what was wrong in my life, what I had hung on to long after I should have let go. I made a promise to change that." She advanced on him until they were both in the hallway again, then poked her finger into his chest and said,

"You? You won't even consider that you can change anything. That people have the power to change, that God can do wonderful work through them. That even where there is great pain, love can—"

"Indoor voices!" Briskly, a familiar figure came hurrying down the narrow corridor.

April retreated inside the doorway again, head bowed as if she suddenly found her feet the single most interesting objects on the planet. "Dr. Joyce, I… We…"

"Don't tell me." The doctor threw her hand up. "I don't need to know. I'm just on my way in to check on Cora and sign her out."

"Just like that?" April asked.

"Don't see why not. This is an emergency room. According to her chart and the doctor on duty, she's not having an emergency, so they don't intend to keep her around."

"So the old gal's all right?" Kurt asked.

"Yup. Bet you'll be glad to get out of here." She slapped Kurt on the arm, then gave April something between a wave and a salute. "I hope you don't mind, but I ordered an ambulance to take her home because of the weather and all. Because it's not an emergency, you won't be able to ride in there with her."

Kurt exhaled. Funny, he hadn't even realized he'd been holding his breath. He scratched the back of his neck, directed his attention to the hallway and called to Dr. Joyce, "Thanks. I'll see that April gets home."

"Don't bother," April said. "I can call someone to come and get me."

"Don't be ridiculous."

"Oh, so now I'm pathetic and ridiculous?"

"You're blowing this way out of proportion." And though he hated to admit it, he was sort of glad she was. The more worked up she got about all this, the happier she'd be to see him hit the bricks.

And he wanted to hit the bricks. *Really.*

"I need to go see my patient." Dr. Joyce headed down the hallway. "Just remember, guys, indoor voices."

"Don't worry. We're done talking anyway."

April opened her mouth, but he didn't let her get a word out.

"C'mon. We can wait outside Miss Cora's door. That way, when Dr. Joyce is done, we can poke our heads in, say goodbye and get going." He reached for her arm.

She yanked it away. "Don't you touch me."

In a few steps, she was down the hallway, matching strides with the doctor.

"Don't be so hard on him, April. It's a big deal that he came here at all, you know."

Kurt considered yelling out "Hey, who needs to use her indoor voice now?" but figured that would only turn both of them against him. And he had enough trouble with women one at a time.

"No, I don't know." He could practically see April

rolling her eyes at the very suggestion. She'd responded like someone who didn't care to know, not like someone breathless to gather information.

That response mattered to Kurt.

"You don't know about Kurt Muldoon and emergency rooms?" Dr. Joyce flipped open the chart in her hand and tsked. "Then you must be the only person in Wileyville who doesn't."

"Doesn't what?"

"Doesn't need to stick her nose in this." Kurt had caught up with them. "You two were only a few steps ahead of me, you know. I could hear every word you said. And it seems to me, Dr. Joyce, my mother wasn't the only one in your office who didn't know how to keep a confidence."

"You are not my patient, Sheriff."

Whack. The metal chart smacked against his midsection.

"If you were, I'd advise you to have your hearing *checked*. Because I didn't divulge anything about you to anyone. Now, if you'll excuse me." She slipped through the glass door and into Miss Cora's room.

"I suppose if I asked you to tell me what that was all about, you'd just glower and say that my knowing wouldn't change anything."

He didn't say a word.

"Okay. Message received. You know what? I'm going to find a pay phone and see if Sadie can come

get me. We'll need to stop by Ezra's Holler to get my
things and my car, if you don't mind."

And if he did mind?

Worse, if he couldn't get the idea of her in his
house, of the time they had shared there, out of his
mind?

He tightened his jaw and shook his head. "Don't
bother your sister. I have to go out there to get
Matilda, and I want to make sure the fire in the fireplace hasn't heated up again. You may as well ride
with me."

She nodded and kept her peace.

If peace was what you could call what settled
between them.

They did not speak.

Not in the corridor.

Not in Miss Cora's room.

Not in his truck on the ride to Ezra's Holler.

Kurt liked it that way.

It suited his plans.

Let her stew. Let her steam. Let her stay mad for
as long as she could, and when that all blew over,
he'd be gone, moved out to his isolated new home.

He didn't owe her any explanation. If she had
really forgiven him, she wouldn't need one.

Besides, he'd made a promise many years ago. He
would not speak to anyone about Carol and what had
happened during those weeks leading up to her
death. Or that last horrible, gut-wrenching night.

And he would not make an exception, not just to ease his conscience.

His conscience did not deserve ease.

The truck rumbled up the driveway.

In a few minutes, they would be at his house. April would hop out of his truck, run inside to gather her things and flee in her car. He might not see her again for a long time. He certainly wouldn't have another chance to tell her.

"It's because of my wife."

"What?" She turned in the unlit cab of his truck, her face illuminated by the glow from the headlights.

"That's why I hate emergency rooms. My wife, Carol, died in one."

"Oh, I—I didn't know, Kurt." The palpable anguish in her tone confirmed her declaration. She had not known. Of all the people in town who had heard and repeated and embellished the story, April was not one of them.

That made parting with her tonight all the harder.

"I'm so sorry. I mean, I guess I knew that you had lost your wife, but I never thought…"

Lost his wife. What a perfect way to put it.

He had lost Carol. Long before the night that she'd had that terrible car accident. He had lost her to another man. No, worse than that—he had lost her because of his own pride and actions.

And he had decided that he would never let that happen again.

Here, in this small, closed space, with no light to show the emotions playing on their faces, he came so close to confessing it all.

What did April say Miss Cora called it? *A hurt you've been carrying inside. Something you can't forgive yourself for and so you can't move past it.*

But what could he do? He couldn't change the past. He could only do everything within his power to control the future.

"I don't want to talk about it," he said finally.

"I know it was hard for you to tell me even that much."

"Yeah."

In the darkness, her hand found his. She gave his fingers a squeeze. "Which is why I know it could never have worked out between us."

She opened the car door and slid her feet to the ground, her touch pulling away slowly until she was outside, looking in.

"Be happy, April," he whispered.

She nodded once, then hurried up the walk to the house where Kurt would soon spend the rest of his life—alone but safe.

Chapter Twelve

"Nobody likes me, everybody hates me, I'm going out in the garden and eat worms." The song just wasn't the same without Miss Cora. April sighed.

She jabbed her gardening tool into the dirt and sat down on the curb that portioned off the strip of land from the parking lot behind her building.

One week until Easter. More like six days, really, if you considered that Sunday was half spent.

Spent. Now there was a word for April.

More than half her life was already spent, not to mention how coming to grips with her own lack of forgiveness had left that good-girl pent-up energy all but spent. April hadn't realized how much she'd relied on that energy to get her through her days.

Cranky customers? They didn't bother her before because, well, they *bothered* her. So she had gotten herself in gear and done something about it.

Likewise with her family. It was so much easier to cope with family if you never actually let yourself stop and think about how much they meant to you.

But thanks to Miss Cora, April no longer had that luxury. Now she had to look at people as they were: people. Not family. Not customers. Not annoyances or problems to be solved or folks to put up a guard against. April had stripped away her own pretenses and suddenly saw that she was not the only person around who struggled every day to keep her inner hurt from showing, to keep it from defining her.

Not just her.

Not just Kurt Muldoon.

"Kurt." She murmured his name and stared at the garden tool sticking up from the dry, barren dirt. She might have come full circle since the last day she sat in the dirt and sang about worms, but she had not ended up in the same place. She had moved on at last.

Her insecurities did not control her anymore. The same could not be said for Kurt.

She shook the dust from the garden tool.

Kurt had moved out to Ezra's Holler full-time. Or that was what she supposed. Sadie had phoned last night to say the sheriff had tendered his resignation effective as soon as the mayor could appoint a replacement, and when a committee of concerned citizens had dropped by his apartment, they found him gone and the place empty.

"Why are you telling me all this?" April had asked.

"Because I thought you might want to know," her sister had replied.

"Or you thought I might already know what *you* want to know. Like, where's he gone? Like, why'd he do it?"

"Like, is he at your house?" Sadie had asked.

"Sadie!" Even now, April bristled at her sister's presumption. April wasn't a prude, and she certainly was old enough to have a gentleman visitor in her home on a Saturday night without a chaperone. And even if he had been with her, nothing untoward would have been going on because she wasn't that kind of girl, and even if she was, she and Kurt were over. Done. Kaput. Finito. "What kind of question is that?" she demanded.

"Obviously the wrong kind, judging by the tone of your voice."

"Thank you."

"So let me ask you this then. Did you chop his body up and use it for fertilizer for the garden?"

"Stop it right now."

"Hey, the man you love with all your heart and, at the same time, wish you could whop over the head with a spade to knock some sense into just went missing. I figure he either came to his senses—with or without help from friendly Mr. Spade—showed up at your door and asked you to run away and marry him, or—"

"Or *I* came to *my* senses and did the poor man in?"

"Ha-ha." Sadie had let out her best imitation of a sinister B-movie mad scientist's laugh. "Now you're thinking like a Shelnutt."

Thinking like a Shelnutt. Three weeks ago, that remark would have cut through her like an Arctic wind. Instead of sisterly camaraderie, she'd have heard, 'Now you're thinking like one of us'—in it. Not one of us. Not really a Shelnutt. Only a Shelnutt stepdaughter. The outsider. 'The one we only keep around because she knows our darkest secrets.'

Why anyone put up with her three weeks ago or all those years before was beyond April. She must have been a real killjoy.

April had laughed lightly. "I'm not sure, is thinking like a Shelnutt a good thing? Or should I seek help immediately?"

"Seek help? Honey, you *are* this family's help."

"No, Sadie. Not anymore. I'm afraid from now on, this family has to grow up and help itself."

"No full armor of God? No girded loins?"

"Always. But for the right reasons now."

"You know what you should do?"

"No, but you're going to tell me, right?"

"You should get yourself a new Bible verse."

"Hmm."

"You know, I picked one out for myself and so did Hannah, sort of our way of proclaiming we've grown up in the Lord. We've changed. We've—"

"Bloomed," April had whispered into the mouthpiece.

"Huh?"

"Blossomed?" she said loud and clear, which hadn't sounded any better than her first choice of descriptions. She had shrugged, then said in her firmest wrapping-up-now tone, "Anyway, I know exactly what you mean, and I'll give it some thought for sure."

"That's all I ask."

April hadn't been able to let that comment go. "That is *so* not all you ask, Sadie."

"Oh, yeah, right, I was asking if you know what's going on with Kurt."

Today, hindsight being what it was, April knew she should have wrapped up the call when the wrapping was good.

"Hon? You still there?" Sadie had asked.

"Yes, I'm here. I'm *always* here."

"And Kurt?" Sadie had seemed determined to trick a confession out of her older half sister.

As if she didn't know that April had given up keeping secrets.

"You want to know about Kurt?" April had put her hand on her hip. No, Sadie could not see that defensive posture, but it had given her voice just the right *oomph* for waiting one, two, three beats before saying "Why don't you ask his mother?"

A choked squeak had answered her.

Yes, in April's new frame of mind, even Lollie Muldoon seemed like a person who deserved understanding. "She's not that bad. In fact, I think she's a very lonely person. Maybe if you reached out to her…"

"I suppose, but—" *Click-click.* "Oops, hold on, call on the other line."

"Sadie, I don't want to—"

Silence. Then "Hey, you'll never guess who that was on the other line!"

Kurt? April hadn't dared to give her hope a voice, so she'd made the next logical leap. "Lollie Muldoon."

"Lollie Mul—hey, you couldn't hear our conversation, could you?"

"No."

"Oh, that's too bad, actually, because she had a message concerning the COCW."

"What? An emergency meeting to track down her son, bloodhounds and helicopters optional?"

"Meeting, yes. Bloodhounds, no."

"They're really calling a meeting to look for Kurt?"

"No. I mean, I don't think so. They probably just want everyone to report how they've done with their projects—you know, with the end of the season coming up Easter Sunday."

"Projects?" Her whole body had tensed. "Thanks but *no thanks*."

"Hey, you have nothing to be ashamed about. You did plenty of good these past few weeks—more than most of us have actually accomplished. My project, for example, was a total failure. Unless you're sure Kurt isn't over there?"

"Yes."

"Okay then. Total failure."

She'd known she shouldn't have asked. Should have just said goodbye and hung up. "Sadie, what *was* your project?"

"Getting you and Kurt together."

April had almost dropped the phone. *Her own sister?* "Sadie! How could you?"

"Brilliantly. Of course." And then she'd laughed. Sadie's laugh could take the sting out of even her most aggravating actions. "I let him think that we all thought he had taken on his own project in taking care of—"

"Me."

"You *and* Miss Cora but, yeah, you."

If April had had a brick wall in her apartment, she'd have gone directly to it and begun banging her head against it. "Go back a second, Sadie—you *let* him think that? You mean, nobody on the COCW ever actually thought that Kurt—"

"Took you on as his project? No." Again with the angst-easing laughter. "April, these are your friends, girl. These are women who *know* you. These are women who, well, apologies for any slight to the male gender, know *men*."

"Uh-huh."

"Not one of them thought for a moment that you didn't have everything with Miss Cora under complete control. The very idea that you needed big, strong, pigheaded Kurt Muldoon in his he-man pickup truck to run to your rescue—"

"Nobody ever pitied me?" she'd rushed to interrupt, needing to make sure she got the point.

"Pity? Well, we did cringe some at the idea of you out there eating your own cooking."

"You must have me confused with Hannah." Their younger sister once suggested that they presoak some chicken—she'd meant marinate. And she'd almost served a cake to her son's soccer team that was partially iced in spackling compound. Compared to her, April deserved airtime on the Food Network. "I am not a bad cook."

"It's true. You're not. You're actually a great cook."

"Thank you."

"If you'd just cook something edible once in a while."

"I'm hanging up now."

"Will you be at the meeting tomorrow afternoon?"

"No."

"You can bring a hot dish."

"After you insulted the things I cook?"

"I promise to eat every bite on my plate and make really loud yummy noises."

"Not even then."

"Aw, April, why not?"

"Busy," she'd said.

"Doing?" her sister had countered.

April had puffed up her chest, glanced out the back window at the unkempt plot of dirt that was her garden and said firmly, "I'm going out in the garden and eat worms."

"Okay, *don't* bring a hot dish."

Click.

True to her word, shortly after church, April had slipped into a pair of white overalls, tied her hair up, stuck a big, floppy gardening hat on her head and gotten down to it. "Big, fat, juicy ones, itty-bitty slimy ones, let's all go eat—"

"Uh, April?"

A long shadow fell across her.

She shivered but did not look up.

"Worms." She finished the song, weakly, but she did finish.

He bent at the knees, bringing himself down to her level. "Sorry to intrude, but—"

"Since you wouldn't come to the meeting, he insisted we bring the meeting to you." Claudia Addams, fresh from Sunday services by the look of her impeccable outfit, came into view on the other side of the median, her heels sounding a hard, precise, no-nonsense rhythm on the concrete of the parking lot.

April narrowed one eye on the man squatting beside her. Her pulse pounded to find him suddenly so close that she could see a nick in his freshly shaven jaw. She wet her lips and forced a grin. "Since when did you become a member of the COCW?"

"I didn't actually." He grinned, too.

April pulled her hat off, hoping to escape the sense of intimacy that the shadow of the brim had created between them.

"Your sister did suggest I join, but we agreed I didn't fit the profile."

"Or the pumps." Sadie moved to stand by her friend Claudia. "Mighty big shoes to fill on this council, you know."

"No, I asked the ladies to break before lunch and come over here as a favor to me." He looked down and to the side for a moment, then raised his head again, uncertainty in his green eyes. "Actually, to you."

April forced her breathing to remain soft and steady. "Me?"

"It's for you, April. I wouldn't do this or anything like it for anyone else, anywhere else, ever."

"Well, at least, you have an open mind about it," Sadie interjected.

April shot her sister a look.

Sadie suddenly looked upward and all but whistled to feign innocence in the whole matter.

"Like I said," Kurt began again.

"Before you do." April put her hand out. She might not have liked what the man had done—or *thought* he had done, more precisely—but he had had the decency to tell her to her face about her being his supposed benevolence project. He had not allowed the potential embarrassment to compound by allowing her to find out in a big way in front of a whole lot of people. Or even just a few people with very big mouths. She owed him the same courtesy.

Okay, courtesy was not really the issue here.

She still really, really cared about the guy, and she wanted to rush to his protection. That was it. Her heart ached for him. More so since she understood what it meant to carry something deep inside year after year until it began to shape not just your thinking but your day-to-day life, as well.

She'd have thrown herself in front of a train to save him; why not run headlong into the path of the COCW for his sake instead?

"Kurt, you really don't have to do this."

"Yes, I do." He took her hand.

Her heart raced.

He wasn't on bended knee, but for one split second, she thought he might ask her to marry him. Hey, a proposal issued from a squatting position was still valid in every state in the union. Ask any woman.

"April…"

One look at the pain still buried deep in his eyes and April knew a proposal just wasn't going to happen. He had come to finally finish things between them, not start something new.

Just like the lilies and the dogwood, we have to clear away all that is no longer useful to us before the Lord can really begin to work in us and help us bloom.

She thought of Miss Cora's wisdom. He needed to find closure so that he could move on. If she let him confess in front of these women something they never even thought he'd done in the first place, that would not bring closure; it would open up a whole new can of worms!

"Kurt, you once told me that you appreciated my help." She leaned forward, resting her hand on his shoulder to command his full attention. She had come a long way and forgiven much, but how could she totally skip the opportunity to throw in one thing? "Which we both know actually meant that you *needed* my help, but you are never going to tell me or anyone that you *need* me, so…"

He turned his head to catch her with a glare. "You have a point here?"

"Yes. My point is, don't do this. Don't make a public scene. Not for me."

"You are the only person I *would* do this for, April."

"And knowing that, the gesture alone is enough."

"I hope you didn't drag us all out of Owtt's so we could watch you sit in the dirt and swap secrets with our garden girl, son." Lollie shaded her eyes.

"Yeah, make with the show, big brother. Apologize or propose or confess something awful already so I can get back inside and put my poor feet up." Still-pregnant Pat bent forward and looked downward. "Assuming I still *have* feet." She winced in the general direction of her mother. "I do still have feet, don't I?"

"Yes, and they are swollen up something miserable." Lollie patted her daughter's back. "Looks like foot problems run in the family today, though. Your brother seems to have grown feet of clay."

"Hey, both of you, zip it."

The looks his sister and mother gave Kurt practically sizzled.

He glowered back. "And stop with the proposal-or-whatever talk. You're only trying to stir things up. I know that you—and all the ladies—believe that the only reason I kept tabs on April and Miss Cora was because I felt—"

"Kurt?" April had to put an end to this. For her own sake now as much as his. "Listen to me," she whispered. "According to Sadie, the ladies didn't actually believe I was your project. In fact, they never gave up making you theirs."

"Me? Theirs? How?"

"By having you think *they* thought you were

taking care of me so that you would spend lots of time doing just that and that would lead to…you know."

She could practically see the pieces of the puzzle fitting together in his mind as his eyes shifted from April to Claudia to Sadie, then out toward his sister and mother standing in the lot, and finally to the handful of other ladies clustered around them.

"They don't know I bought Ezra's Holler, do they?" he whispered.

"They didn't hear it from me."

"Good. If you need to get in touch with me, you know where to find me." He stood, his hands wide, and finally and loudly addressed the crowd. "Well, forget what you believed. I did it because I felt like it. There. It needed to be said. And I said it."

He turned to April and extended his hand.

She rose and slid her hand in his.

Take me with you, she said with her eyes.

He shook her hand.

No. She knew it wouldn't happen. He had too much deadwood inside. And only he could tend to that. Only Kurt and the Lord could prepare his heart to love again.

She leaned over their clasped hands. "You know, of course, that what you've just done is going to get you talked about."

"Yeah?" He smiled. If they had been alone, he might have even planted a quick kiss on her cheek. "Better me than you."

She mouthed the words "Thank-you" and stepped back.

"Ladies—" he tipped his head "—sorry for any inconvenience. Please, go back to your meeting. And Claudia?"

Mrs. Addams stood with her arms crossed and her toe tapping.

"Send the bill for everyone's meal to me, care of my mother's address, won't you?"

"Oh, I will. Don't you worry about that. I will send you that bill, Sheriff. *For everyone's meal.* And I believe I, for one, will be having dessert."

"Me, too!"

"A whole pie, thank you very much."

"*And* an appetizer."

The murmuring started then, reaching its peak seconds before Kurt made it to the door of his pickup.

April didn't know whether to laugh or cry or join in the free-food ordering frenzy.

On the one hand, Kurt had made this wonderful, amazing, most-difficult-thing-in-the-world-for-him gesture. It totally negated her assumption that he had preyed upon her weaknesses and vulnerability by trying to force her to keep their love a secret. On the other hand, the man was walking away.

For good.

Leaving her literally in the dirt.

With the worms.

And the COCW.

She hadn't thought the day could get any worse.

Then the radio in Kurt's truck crackled to life and she found out how wrong she had been.

Chapter Thirteen

Lollie Muldoon reckoned they just might have witnessed God's handiwork, that call coming in when it did.

The dispatcher had barely signed off with the news that Miss Cora had fallen ill and been taken to the hospital when Lollie collected every last one of the council women into a prayer circle.

"Go. You two go and see what you can do," she ordered her son and April. "We have our own work here. Tell Miss Cora she's covered in our prayers."

Kurt held the passenger side door of his pickup open for April and gave his mother and all the women assembled a nod.

"And call me as soon as you know something," Lollie demanded. "I mean that!"

They tore out of the parking lot and headed toward the local hospital. Not the bigger, better-equipped one two towns over, where they could run tests and take extreme measures to save Miss Cora's life if the need arose.

April did not need Dr. Joyce present to tell her that things did not bode well. And yet, she wasn't worried.

"It's not actually so bad, is it?"

"I don't know how bad Miss Cora is. The dispatcher was just relaying what she'd gotten on the scanner from the ambulance drivers."

"No, not Miss Cora. It's not so bad living in a town where people sometimes know a little too much about your business. Not at a time like this."

"I don't follow you."

"Well, consider Miss Cora. Something bad happens and the dispatcher makes a call because she knows it matters to you and within moments half the people Miss Cora knows are praying for her. And when they're done, they'll contact everyone they know and pretty soon half the county will be praying for Miss Cora, too. Wileyville's not so bad when you look at it that way, is it?"

Kurt didn't say a word. He just kept driving and within two minutes they were at the hospital.

Things happened so fast that night. The hospital staff rushed Miss Cora here, then there. Blood was drawn. Tests and more tests were conducted. And waiting. Lots and lots of waiting.

April filled the hours with prayer. Kurt, too,

though he did not offer to pray with her and she did not ask. It seemed too…too personal a gesture. One he'd have to make himself.

And he didn't.

So April was on her own that way. On her own but not alone, as she knew so many people all over the county were joining with her in asking the Lord to watch over His sweet, faithful servant.

By morning, they had moved Miss Cora to a room and could only say, "We hope to know more soon."

After that, the hours went by slowly, yet the days seemed to elapse in quick succession.

On Monday and Tuesday, nurses and technicians came and went from Miss Cora's room.

April passed the time, telling Miss Cora what was happening at the store. The COCW volunteers who were running it for her had bought so many items that it looked as if she'd have her best spring quarter ever. She even read from the Bible and, at one point, carried on a one-sided discussion about the verse her father had chosen for her as a child and Sadie's insistence that she find a new one for the next phase of her life.

On Wednesday, Miss Cora opened her eyes but did not recognize anyone.

On Thursday, April asked Kurt to bring in the biggest, fattest tomato he could find from the grocery store. Miss Cora smiled when she saw it, then…nothing. Maybe April had imagined the smile?

"Why don't you bring in a dogwood branch to-morrow?" she asked on Friday night when Kurt made her leave the room to go down to the cafeteria for something to eat. "They're in bloom now," she said as they approached the elevator, "and you know how much she'd love to see—"

Kurt pointed to a sign beside the elevator: Heart and Lung Wing. No Live Plants or Cut Flowers Beyond This Point.

On Saturday, it rained. April didn't mind. It matched her mood.

She entered Miss Cora's room, head down, umbrella in one hand, coat over her arm and a stack of reading material to get her through the afternoon, when the only voice she would hear would be—

"'The Lord will guide you always. He will satisfy your needs in a sun-scorched land and will strengthen your frame. You will be like a well-watered garden, like a spring whose waters never fail.'"

"Miss Cora! You're awake!"

She nodded once. "Isaiah 58:11."

"I, uh, Isaiah? I'm not sure…"

"You wanted a new verse for yourself."

"You heard that?"

Another nod, this time a little more enthusiastically. "Woke up this morning with that on my mind, so I had the nurse look it up to make sure I got it right."

"And you did." April had no doubts, just as she

could not doubt her joy at finding her old friend on the mend again.

"Think you should consider it for your own."

"I will." April walked to the bedside, leaned in and kissed her thin-skinned cheek.

Dry lips smacked back, grazing her on the ear. Old hands gripped her arms tightly and kept her from pulling away before Miss Cora could command eye contact and demand "Where's my tomatoes, girl?"

"I'll bring you some tomorrow."

And she drifted off.

April moved to stand at the window and watch the rain falling gently over her beloved little hometown.

The Lord will guide you always. He will satisfy your needs in a sun-scorched land...

April liked it.

You will be like a well-watered garden, like a spring whose waters never fail.

Even if she didn't think it fit her entirely.

She pushed at the curtains to open them wider and spoke to her friend, even though she did not think she would answer. "Miss Cora, I just have one question for you."

"Only the one?"

April turned to find her aged eyes open again, her trembling lips in a faint smile.

"When you get stronger, I'll have more," she promised. "For now, I only wonder, how will I know when I bloom?"

"Can you hear the lilies of the field asking such a thing?"

"No."

"Then you shouldn't, either. But since you have…" She held out her hand.

April took it, as she sat on the edge of the bed.

"You'll know when you're ready."

"Ready?" April felt she had lived her entire life ready. Ready for her mother to return. Ready for her sisters to stop bickering. Ready to find a man she preferred sharing her Saturdays with more than she would a virus. But her mother was never coming back. Her sisters had not only stopped bickering but also stopped needing her. And when she had found that man? Well, she didn't think it was *her* lack of readiness for the relationship that kept them apart. "Ready for what, Miss Cora?"

"Ready to open up. Ready to cast aside your fears and trust what the Lord has in store for you, whatever that might be. Like a flower isn't afraid of the sun *or* the rain."

April wanted to protest. Afraid? Her?

Yes, her.

Most certainly.

Fear had held her back from so many things. Fear of harming her family if she spoke the truth. Fear of people not liking her if she spoke her mind. Fear of losing Kurt if she spoke up about anything.

Forgiving wasn't the last step; it was the first.

Miss Cora had tried to tell her that, but April hadn't been ready to hear it. Forgiveness prepared the way for God to work in her.

And when she could let go of her fears…

"No other questions?"

"Not, uh, not now." She had a lot to absorb with the answer to just this one.

"Good. Then I have one for you." Miss Cora closed her eyes and swallowed, and for a moment, April wondered if she had fallen asleep again. Then she blinked, smiled and asked, "Where's your young man?"

"My, oh, Kurt?" She turned her face toward the rain-streaked window and said absently, "He mostly comes by at night, I think. Usually after normal visiting hours. He's still the sheriff, so nobody bothers him. Nobody says anything to him. Neither do I."

So that was how April would sum up his life, Kurt thought, hanging back by the open door just out of sight of the two women.

Nobody bothers him. Nobody says anything to him.

That was what he'd had in mind since the day he first considered buying the house at Ezra's Holler. He should be proud of himself. He'd done it. He'd gotten exactly what he wanted.

Then why, when he looked in at the woman caring for the sweet old lady in the hospital bed, did he feel as if he'd lost everything?

He took a deep breath, plastered on a grin and went inside. "Well, look who finally decided to open her eyes!"

"There he is!" Miss Cora held open her arms to him.

"Kurt?" April leapt up from the edge of the bed. "What are you doing here?"

"My sister had her baby a few hours ago." He tried not to notice the rush of redness in April's cheeks, the way his very presence seemed to make her hands unable to stay still, flitting from her braid to her buttons to the bed rail and back again. Funny that he should make her so nervous when she had just the opposite effect on him. Over these past few days, alone at his new house, he had felt restless and unsettled. But the minute he walked into this room and laid eyes on her… Calm. Peace.

He exhaled and walked to the side of the bed across from April. "I came down to see my new nephew."

"A baby!" Miss Cora clapped her hands together so softly that they hardly made a sound. "Oh, my, that *is* better than a tomato in my book any day!"

"Tomato?" He cocked his head at April.

She pointed to the one on the window ledge.

He nodded. "Well, at least with a tomato, you don't have to worry about saving for college."

"But a tomato won't help you when you're old and ill." Miss Cora sighed.

"I don't know. It might make you some soup." April smiled.

Kurt groaned.

Miss Cora said, "I like soup. But I do admit, I like babies better. When are you two having some?"

"Soup?" April asked.

"Babies!" Cora swatted the air. Clearly, if either one of them had been within reach, she'd have preferred to make contact with them.

"Miss Cora, Kurt and I are not—"

He held his hand up. Why go through all that with the old dear? Besides, he'd have enough to replay in his mind—all the missed opportunities, all the things he'd never realize with April without having to hear her say it.

He dropped a kiss on Miss Cora's forehead and said, "You get better soon enough and we'll wheel you up to the nursery window to take a look."

Miss Cora jabbed a crooked finger in April's direction. "You go take a peek for me now."

April lifted her eyes to meet his in a questioning glance.

He nodded. "Sure. Go. I'll stay here and keep Miss Cora company."

"Baby-sit me, you mean." She shifted in the bed, wincing from even the slightest movement. "You save that for the babies."

"Just one baby, Miss Cora. Kurt's nephew." April retrieved her purse and rounded the bed. "We'll be back in a— Miss Cora?"

But she had gone Home.

Half an hour later, after Kurt had made the necessary phone calls and signed all the appropriate paperwork, he found April standing in the hallway with her back against the wall.

"Do you...do you want me to take you to the hospital chapel?" he asked.

She raised her red-rimmed eyes to his and shook her head. "I think I'd rather go and see your new nephew."

A lump rose in his throat. "Really?"

"Yes." She nodded and, to his amazement, smiled—that shy, sweet smile that had won his heart the very first time he saw it. "I think Miss Cora would've liked that. For us to go and lay our eyes on the very beginning of a life here in these hours after..."

She couldn't finish.

He drew her into his arms and laid his cheek on the top of her head. "If you're sure."

"Honestly, I can't think of anywhere else I'd rather be." She stepped back. "Or anyplace more appropriate to go and celebrate the life of Cora Mae Barrett, whose work is done."

Chapter Fourteen

Easter morning dawned the way it can only in Kentucky: warm and still. Wisps of fog clung to the low ground between the hills, like lingering smoke from a smoldering campfire.

April was in her best dress and shoes she didn't mind getting damp with dew. She'd worn a sweater for the walk to the sunrise service out near the old cemetery, but by the time the first pink light stretched up over the sky above Wileyville she slipped it off. Standing with her friends and family gathered around, she sang of the risen Lord, of hope and joy and life reborn. In prayer, she poured out her gratitude for Miss Cora, for her own life and, most of all, for the blood of Christ.

It was perfect and peaceful and gorgeous. The only place she could imagine it being more beautiful was Ezra's Holler.

When the service concluded, her father handed her one perfect white lily. She kissed him on the cheek and said, "Daddy, what would you think if I picked a new Bible verse to guide and uplift me?"

"I'd think it was long overdue, child." He took her hand. "I chose that verse for you because, of all my girls, you were the one I wanted to protect the most. Hannah and Sadie, they were mine by blood. No one could take them away from me. But you? I felt I never knew how much time I would have with you. I wanted you to know from a very young age and never, ever forget that you and God were strong enough together. That He would be your shelter even if I couldn't be."

"Oh, Daddy." She touched his face. "I do know that. In fact, I've chosen a verse that reflects that and my new hope for my life from this point forward."

"Oh?"

"Isaiah 58:11. 'The Lord will guide you always. He will satisfy your needs in a sun-scorched land and will strengthen your frame. You will be like a well-watered garden, like a spring whose waters never fail.'" She pressed her lips together, trying to keep the joy that saying it gave her from spilling out and seeming, well, unseemly.

"Wonderful!" Solomon "Moonie" Shelnutt slapped his hands together and laughed hard and loud and so boisterously that heads turned to see what commotion he'd stirred up now.

Count on her daddy to know just the right response. And to follow it up with just the right question: "And now what, darling April?"

"Now?"

"You said this was for your life from this point forward. Can't go forward by standing here and sticking your feet in the ground. All you can get that way is rootbound."

"Rootbound," she whispered, amazed at her father's insightful encouragement.

"Shake off the dirt from those feet, girl. Are you ready?"

Ready? For what? She didn't have to ask. April knew.

To bloom.

"Yes, Daddy," she murmured. And she knew exactly where she had to go and what she had to do.

"Don't look at me that way. I know it's Easter. I know I should be getting dressed for church. But if you were a different breed of dog, not the bossy kind of breed who tries to herd everyone into the right place at the right time, you'd realize I have a church not one hundred yards away from my back door."

Matilda snorted.

It wasn't an opinion, Kurt knew. Matilda was a dog. She didn't care when or how he worshiped God; she only cared that her food bowl was full and her tummy got rubbed as often as possible. But deep down, *he* knew. And a snort was just the kind of incredulous response his remark deserved.

Not to mention the only response he was likely to get now or for a very long time, since the only people who knew where he had gotten himself to this last week had strict instructions to let him be.

"Which is exactly what I want," he told the dog.

Another snort.

"Well, if you're going to be that way, I'm heading outside. *Alone.*" Why he felt compelled to tack that on, Kurt didn't know.

Alone. It was the way he did everything these days. The way he would go on doing things for a very long time to come.

He stepped out onto the porch, where he had kissed April and held her in his arms on that snowy night not so long ago.

"It's called a dogwood winter," she had told him.

Dogwood winter. A reminder that spring is a promise that doesn't always come easily. *And* that the cold doesn't have to last. All things are far too brief in this life and only love is eternal.

Kurt so wanted to believe that, to know it for his own life.

He so wanted to believe.

He tucked his hands in his jean pockets, drew his shoulders up and took in a deep breath. His chest ached. Sunlight stung his eyes. He'd gotten everything he said he wanted—and now he wanted to believe that he could have just a little bit more.

From his vantage point, he could see the road that led past his long driveway. The one he'd watched April take when she returned to Wileyville once and for all.

If he walked a few feet to his right, he could see the garden where he had brushed April's hair. The place where he had planted the lilacs. The garden he had pledged to care for when April had gone.

A few steps to his left and he would be able to see the side of his house, where Miss Cora had gotten stuck in the window. And the dogwood, now in bloom, its very pale white-and-pink blossoms telling the story of redemption. The markings of the cross.

And beyond that, the church, the school, the jail—an entire would-be town with a population of one.

Matilda came to the door and whined.

"Ezra's Holler. Population: One man, one dog."

"And plenty of room to grow."

"April!" Had he been so lost in thought that he hadn't heard her drive up? "How did…where's your car?"

"I parked by the road and walked up so I could pick these along the way." She showed him a bundle of colorful wildflowers and greenery bunched around a single white lily.

"They're beautiful."

She was beautiful. The very sight of her filled his

heart and chased away the ache. Everything he'd ever wanted—and a little bit more.

He descended the steps and walked toward her. "Do you want to come inside and put those flowers in water?"

She held them under her nose and raised her eyes to his. "You mean you don't want to chase me off for intruding on your private sanctuary?"

No, he did not want to chase her off. He wanted to find a reason for her to stay. *Forever.*

But he didn't say that. "I, uh, I figured you'd come out here for something you'd forgotten."

"Yeah, I did." She stepped close to him, a light in her eyes he hadn't seen for a while.

"What?" he asked softly.

"This." She went on tiptoe, raised her arms to put her hands on his shoulders and placed a single sweet kiss on his waiting lips.

He had hoped against all hope that was what she had forgotten. And he'd dreaded it, too. Neither winter nor spring, he was in his own perpetual dogwood winter until…

The kiss was so tender and yet so intense. So innocent. So fleeting.

She stepped back, her gaze never leaving his.

"I forgot that, Kurt. And to say good-bye."

"I've had goodbye kisses before, April. That was *not* a goodbye kiss."

"Yes, it was." She wore her hair loose today, and a

strand blew across the impromptu bouquet in her hand. "Goodbye to the old, to the useless, to the things that hold us back and keep us from blossoming."

"April," he murmured.

She put her fingers to his lips to stop him from saying any more. "Goodbye to being afraid, Kurt. Rain or shine, God is good. He is my armor for a wicked day so that I can stand. He is a spring that will never run dry."

"If you came to preach a sermon, the church is that way." He gave a jerk of his head.

"I didn't come to preach to you, Kurt. I came to *speak* to you. At last and without fear of setting you off or of losing you." She set her flowers aside and put her hands on his face.

He swallowed and searched her face, every line and shadow, every freckle and flaw, and all he found was…

"Because, you see, I'm not scared anymore. I'm not so proud that I think my ability to be a good girl and do what everyone else expects of me is the very thing that holds the world together."

"Forgiveness," he whispered. "You're talking about forgiveness."

"Forgiveness is the first step. It's God's way of preparing us to grow. I know that now."

"So you came to tell me that you forgive me?"

"I did that a while ago, Kurt. I came because I'm not afraid to tell you the truth. And the truth is that the reason we can't move forward, the reason we never *could* move forward since the day we met, is that you are hanging on to something inside of you that has died and can't blossom. You have to let it go. You have to forgive yourself."

"For?"

"Even if I knew what for, I couldn't do that for you. And until you can do it for yourself…" She kissed him again, this time on the cheek, then gathered her flowers and, with tears in her eyes, turned and started back down the driveway.

Matilda whined again and scratched to be let out.

He watched her go and, for the first time, *saw* her, really saw the *woman*. Not the girl who made him laugh. Not the person who challenged him intellectually. Not the daughter of Moonie Shelnutt, magnet for local gossip and speculation. Not the caregiver to gardens and great-grandmotherly ladies. But the integration of all of those and more. She was like…

She was a garden come out of winter and in full bloom. And if he didn't step out from under the cold of his own pain, he would lose her forever.

He took a step onto the walkway and called out, "Carol."

She made a half turn, the flowers cradled in her arms. "What?"

Two more steps toward her. "My late wife."

A full turn toward him now. "Yes?"

"That's what I can't forgive myself for." He

stopped and anchored his feet on the walkway. "What I'm hanging on to."

She bridged the last few feet between them with light, delicate steps that made her hair swish softly around her shoulders. "Kurt, if you feel that having a new life would somehow dishonor the love you shared with your wife—"

"No." He put his hand up. "It's *me*."

Her eyebrows creased downward. She shook her head.

"*I* dishonored her, and then she died and I never found a way to make it right." He clenched his jaw and scanned the road that led back to Wileyville. "I couldn't make it right."

"What are you saying? You were unfaithful?" She barely whispered it.

He held her gaze. "You really have to ask that?"

She shook her head.

"No. Not me. Her. You know she was an officer, like me? Well, there was this enlisted guy—very young, very fun, very…" *Everything I never was.* He shook off the memory and shifted his feet on the walkway. "Everyone on the base knew. Everyone was talking behind my back, laughing." He fit his fist into his open palm. "It burned me up. I won't say it didn't because it did."

"Of course, Kurt, anyone would feel that way if a spouse cheated."

"I felt so…" He cut himself off before swearing.

He had done so well between his promise to his mother and his respect for April and Miss Cora. He didn't want to start it again now. Not over this. "I felt so helpless."

"Which you can't stand."

"No kidding." He ground one hand into the other, unable to meet her gaze yet. "That and all the gossip. The humiliation. So I did the only thing I could."

"Left her?" she whispered.

He shook his head.

"What then?"

"Turned the talk against her." His voice had gone dry and tortured. He had never spoken to anyone about this until now. No one had ever asked him about it. No one had blamed him. What had happened had happened. No one had held it against him.

If he hadn't been a man of conscience, a man of faith, he might have picked up his life after his wife died and gone on and never given it another thought. "I told everybody I knew and, more to the point, everybody *she* knew. Told them about the guy, about the affair, about her and all the ways she had failed me and our marriage. She was my *wife* and I—"

"You were hurt and confused."

"Hurt, yes." Hurt still. He forced down the lump in his throat. "Confused? April, have you forgotten where I come from? I have watched my mother systematically push away everybody who loves her, everybody who might have relied on her and whom she might have relied on and all because of her inability to keep her big mouth shut. I know the power of the vicious rumor. I knew exactly what I was doing."

She touched his arm.

He stared at the place where her fingers lay against the wrinkled cotton fabric of his sleeve. "What I hadn't realized was how quickly it would get out of control. Or how far it would go."

"If you didn't know…"

"I *knew*, April." He dropped his arm to break contact with her. "I knew better than to act like that. She was my *wife*. I should have done everything in my power to protect her, not expose her to that kind of scrutiny."

He raised his head and swept the horizon with his gaze. "This was back when there were some very public affairs in the military, when people had their eyes on that kind of thing more than ever. It ended up looking like it would cost both of them their careers. But they were killed in a car accident before that could happen."

"And before you had a chance to work through what you had done."

"You say forgiveness is the first step?" He ran his hands back through his hair. If it made the gray show through, he did not care. If that made him look old or tired or less than the perfect specimen of manhood, well, fine by him. He was all of those things. "I never got the chance to ask for that from her. Not that I deserved it."

"So you spent these last years denying forgiveness to yourself instead."

"I'll be honest with you, April. I don't know how to do it."

"So since you can't figure out how to deal with what you feel inside, you decided to take total control of everything on the outside?"

"I hadn't actually given it that much thought, but you're probably right."

"All of it—coming home to rescue your mom, becoming the sheriff, keeping our relationship hush-hush."

"I'm not the kind of guy who actually uses terms like *hush-hush*," he reminded her. "Look, I'm not some sad sap who beats himself up over some sin he thinks he can never get past."

"No?"

"No. I may not make it to church every Sunday—or any Sunday since I moved back to Wileyville—but I'm not a man who could ever proclaim to follow a faith I didn't understand. I get that I am forgiven. Washed clean. Got it."

"Then why don't you—"

"It's not forgiveness that's lacking in me, April. It's trust."

"You don't trust who? Me?"

"Myself. After what I did, I don't trust myself.

I'm a man who lived his life by analyzing situations, forming plans, following through."

"And your plan was to—"

"Never put myself in a long-term relationship where a few words—some careless talk, gossip, rumor— could betray it all." He brushed her hair back. "I didn't protect Carol, but I was determined to protect you."

"I don't need protection, Kurt. I'm not afraid of what people say. I'm certainly not afraid of you."

"I know." *He knew.* "What I didn't know is, when did you get so smart? You figured it all out for both of us."

"Miss Cora did most of the 'heavy lifting,' as you'd say." She edged closer to him, one blink and just a hint of tears, then a smile. "I sure will miss that old troublemaker."

"Maybe you'd miss her a little less if you could look out and see the dogwood where she got stuck and think of her."

"Yeah, maybe, but I can't see that dogwood from my apartment in Wileyville."

"Yeah?" He put his arm around her shoulders.

She nodded.

"Got a pretty good view of it from that corner of the porch." He took her wrist and gestured toward the location. "And from the back door. And the back window downstairs. The bay window upstairs. The garden. The—"

"Kurt?"

"Hmm?"

"Unless you're offering to deed me this place so I can get a good look at that dogwood when I want to think of Miss Cora, I think you need to ask me something."

He laughed. "Man, you really aren't afraid anymore, are you?"

She put her hand on his cheek. "Why should I be? Rain or shine, God is constant and love *does* change things."

"It certainly does." He took a deep breath. Love had changed him. He couldn't deny it, especially as he moved around in front of the woman he loved and bent down on one knee. "April Shelnutt?"

"Yes." She bent and placed a kiss on his lips. "Yes."

"I love you," he murmured between kisses.

"It's going to cause talk, you know. The town's spinster garden lady marrying the hometown hero."

He put his forehead to hers and shut his eyes. "Marry me and move out here and we won't hear a word of it."

"Not until I fix up the place and the school tours begin and then the church youth-group bonfires. And don't forget the COCW."

He reached down, fit his arm beneath her knees and lifted her in his arms. "How could I ever forget the COCW?"

And he didn't.

How could he? They planned the biggest,

gaudiest wedding ever seen in the whole history of Wileyville for him and April. Inviting everyone Kurt thought he had ever known and a few people he had never even heard of but was assured would be quite insulted if they weren't included in the festivities.

Though when the day came, Kurt felt anything but festive. Claustrophobic was more like it.

That prompted him to pick up the phone on the morning of the wedding and place a call.

Chapter Fifteen

"Let's elope."

April smiled into the phone. Yeah, not even a trained military man and official of the law—at least, for another few weeks until the new sheriff would take over—could *hear* a smile, but somehow she knew that he knew her exact expression when she let out a sympathetic sigh and said, "No can do, babe. We have nearly two hundred people heading toward Ezra's Holler, even as we speak. Even if we wanted to elope, we'd get stuck in all the incoming traffic just trying to make a run for it."

"Yeah, I suppose you're...*two hundred?*"

"Okay, I exaggerate."

Instantly, every eye in the room fixed on her, including both of April's sisters, her future sister-in-law and the baby born just before Miss Cora died and Kurt proposed. April held her hands up in the universal calm-down gesture, then turned her back to the women about to don pastel organza gowns who, with a median age of 40, had dubbed themselves the "world's oldest bridesmaids."

"It's more like one hundred and ninety-something," April told her groom.

"One hundred?" he repeated.

"And ninety-*something*," she finished, a bit too loud and a little too briskly.

"Shh, girl. You'll scare him off. Not even my mother knows the exact count," Pat whispered. Well, whispered the way a person does when that person is on stage and wants even the back row to hear her.

"In my whole lifetime, I haven't even met that many people, have you?"

"I guess both of us in our lifetimes have." April poked her finger in her ear and ignored Pat's input. "And toss in people around town that we didn't want to offend and friends of the family and people coming to help with the catering and cleanup and—"

"The *entire* sheriff's department and their significant others, not to mention kids and stepkids and even grandkids." He would come around. She knew he would. The old April might have worried that the man would size up the size of things and run for his life.

But this was his life now. Their life. And whatever came, rain or shine or one hundred and ninety-plus wedding guests, they would get through it, grow through it.

"Hey, you wait until you're over forty to get married, you rack up a lot of wedding and baby IOUs," she reminded him. "Nobody felt they could turn down this invite. People on both sides of our families have been looking forward to this day for a very long time, you know."

"They aren't the only ones."

He said it all low and sweet, the way he had of talking only to her that—she had discovered over the last few weeks—made her knees turn to jelly and her nerves tingle. Imagine that. At her age, after so many years of keeping up her guard and never letting anyone get too close, she had found a man who could get under her skin with the sound of his voice. Found him, almost lost him and found him again. Forever.

"I know," she murmured into the mouthpiece. "It feels like we've waited forever for this day, but it only took two months to plan it all."

"Spoken as the one—"

"Not doing the heavy lifting?" She laughed lightly at the phrase he had once used to imply that he was bearing the emotional weight of their situation. Turning slowly, she gazed out the window of the back bedroom, where she and her attendants were dressing. "Do I have to remind you who did all the landscaping out here?"

"While I restored the church and did as much cosmetic work on the house as time permitted," he said, and she could tell by his tone that he wanted to hear her tell him he'd done a good job.

"It looks gorgeous," she purred.

"Thanks," Sadie said, doing a spin in her gown.

April smiled. Her sister looked lovely in the floating fabric that draped over her shoulders and skimmed her hips and...didn't quite fasten in the back!

Mouth gaping, April shot a look of panic to Hannah.

Hannah, still in her robe, shrugged and pantomimed a person eating. And eating. And eating.

"April?"

"Hmm?"

"Where are we going to put everybody? The church only holds about a hundred."

April sighed. "Can't you just...try holding your breath and squeezing..."

"The guests?"

"Sadie—" April rolled her eyes "—ordered her dress a size too small, thinking she'd lose ten pounds before the wedding."

"Sadie? In *two* months?" He laughed, not in a mean way but in what she could only describe as a man's way. Giving the impression that a guy never would have done anything so foolish. "With all the punch and cake the women of Wileyville have been pushing at the wedding party?"

"You know me, ever the optimist," Sadie called into the mouthpiece as she came to stand beside April.

April gave her sister a delicate push and stood back to study the situation. "You'd better let me go, Kurt, so I can tend to all of this."

"Still the one holding your family together, huh?"

"The only thing I plan to hold together right now is Sadie's dress."

Kurt sighed. "Help your sister," he said.

"Always."

"April?"

"Hmm?"

"Meet me in the church at two o'clock?"

"I'll be the one in the big white dress."

Hannah took the phone before April could say a proper good-bye and called into it, "Bye, Kurt. You better be nice to my sister or I'll write terrible things about you in my newspaper column."

"He's not afraid of your column, Hannah." Kurt's sister pushed up the sleeves of her white terry-cloth robe and quipped loud enough for her brother to hear, "If he doesn't behave, *I'll* tell our mama."

April seized the phone just in time to hear the sweetest thing she thought the man had ever said. "Tell whoever you want. April and I have no secrets."

"Oh, Kurt," she murmured. "See you in a little over an hour."

"I can't wait."

"Me, either."

"Then let's—"

"We're *not* eloping!" And she hung up.

"You two are too cute," Hannah said as she slipped a sea of petticoats and then the seed-pearl wedding dress over April's carefully curled hair.

"You were just as cute when you got married," Pat reminded the youngest Shelnutt sister.

"You're thinking of my husband." Hannah began to fuss with April's makeup. "He's the cute one in the family."

"I don't know. That son of yours is awfully adorable." Pat handed her own child to Sadie, then all but stuck her knee in the middle of Sadie's back to get the best angle for fastening the stubborn zipper.

"Foster son," Sadie said automatically.

"Not for long," Hannah hurried to say, her eyes alight with the kind of joy only a person who had waited a long, long time to see love fulfilled could recognize.

Everyone in the room froze.

"The adoption is going through at last?" April clapped her hands together, bumping the fat brush from Hannah's hands and sending a cloud of bisque-colored face powder over both of them. She didn't care. She pulled her sister into a hug. Hannah and her husband, Payton, had wanted to adopt their foster son, Sam, for the longest time. Now, apparently, it was happening. "Why didn't you say anything sooner?"

"I didn't want to take away from your big day with our news." Hannah rubbed her nose and squinted as if she wanted to sneeze.

"Take away?" April gave her sister another hug, laughing. "Having our family grow not by one but by two members? I can't think of a better time to announce good news than at my wedding!"

"Sadie, do you have any news *you* want to announce?" Pat asked, even as she teasingly prodded the middle Shelnutt sister's middle.

"I'm going on a diet." Red-faced from the struggle, Sadie handed Pat's baby back and joined in the sisterly embrace.

"I'm getting dressed." Pat set her baby in the carrier and reached for one of two gowns lying across the end of the bed. She picked up one and then the other and turned, her hand on her hip. "Sadie, you're wearing the wrong gown."

"I am?" Sadie looked at them all and blinked, then a slow grin came over her. "In that case, forget the diet. And I do have an announcement to make."

"Oh?"

"Ed sold his business and he's retiring."

"Oh, Sadie, are you happy?" April asked. The pharmacy, known to all as Pickett's on the Point, had sometimes seemed to own Ed rather than vice versa.

"Forget happy." Pat pushed into the group, handing the right gowns to the right women. "Are you going to be rich?"

Sadie laughed. "If it means I get to spend more time with my hubby, then yes, I will be rich beyond my wildest imagination."

More hugs, more zipper tugs and before she could take in all the news and comprehend all the joy in her heart, April stood before the mirror in her wedding gown.

And the door swung open.

"Will you girls stop your gabbing and… Oh, my!" The usual twinkle in Moonie's eyes went misty. His whole face softened into a sweet smile. He went to April with his arms outstretched and took her hands in his. "You're as lovely as a garden in full bloom."

"Love will do that to a person."

He nodded. "Seems like no time at all since I was standing at the end of a church aisle with you walking along tossing rose petals on the path ahead of your precious mama in her wedding outfit." He went quiet and, given his history of what the doctor called mini-strokes, everyone in the room fell silent with him. But he didn't fade on them. Instead, he blinked and in a cracked voice said, "If only…"

"No, Daddy." April wiped away his tears, then let her hand rest on his wrinkled cheek. "This is not a day for if-onlys. This is a day for rejoicing and celebrating. It's not about what might have been but about what is now and what is going to be."

"Yes, yes. Absolutely right, my darling." He

kissed her hand, then took a hankie from his pocket, swiping it under his eyes. "You look so pretty."

"And you look downright dapper, Daddy." She stood back in all her finery, folded her arms and said, "Frisk him, girls."

Hannah and Sadie began checking his pockets and his sleeves.

"No squirting lapel flowers," Sadie reported.

"No joy buzzers," Hannah concluded.

Pat took him by the wrist and raised his arm. "No…"

Dum-dum-da-dum. Dum-dum-da-dum. The tinny electronic notes of "The Wedding March" sounded.

"Cuff links." He held up his arm, grinning at the plastic bell-shaped gadgets on his sleeves.

"And?" April prodded.

He heaved a sigh and reached up to press the knot on his seemingly plain, white silk bowtie.

April gazed at the man who, on the day of his marriage to her mother, had also made a commitment to her. To love and protect, to give her a family that would never be taken from her, no matter what the cost.

And she laughed.

"What? They didn't have a top hat with a glow-in-the-dark hatband to match?"

"Are you daft, girl?"

"Well…"

"Not for a day wedding!"

"Are we just about ready?" Lollie Muldoon bustled into the room—well, as much as a woman of her age and size could bustle. Her silver-blue dress swished along the floor, and no one had the nerve to mention that it matched her fresh-from-the-sink-with-an-at-home-rinse hair color perfectly. "Okay, you've got something old..."

"The bridesmaids!" Pat, Hannah and Sadie all chimed in at once.

"Miss Cora's Bible," April gently corrected them, secretly happy they hadn't said "the bride."

"Something new?"

"My engagement ring?" Kurt had finally gotten around to giving it to her about ten days ago—not that April had missed it. It was prime planting and plant-nurturing season, after all, and she didn't plan to dig in the dirt with a diamond on her finger. Moonie had reminded her that diamonds started out in the ground and it wasn't likely she'd hurt the thing. But since she planned on only having one engagement ring ever, April wanted to keep it pristine—at least, until the wedding. So in the box it had stayed.

"No, you can't use your engagement ring because Kurt has it, remember?"

He'd taken it to the jewelers to have it affixed to her wedding band.

"Your bouquet?" Pat suggested, handing it to her.

"Good enough. Not like we actually put any stock

in these things, so that will do just fine. Except..." Lollie peered at the mix of wildflowers and greenery. "Now how can it be something new with that old thing stuck in there?"

Lollie bent toward the bouquet, her thumb and forefinger poised in a pinch.

"No! Leave it." April covered the broken dogwood twig she had found with Miss Cora's things after the old girl had passed away. "It reminds me of a very dear friend. And of how Kurt and I got together. And that in life and in marriage, sometimes you have to clear away the deadwood in order for God to help you blossom."

Lollie frowned, but she didn't argue. "Something borrowed?"

"Your pearl earrings." April lifted a strand of her hair to show Kurt's mother that she was wearing the family-heirloom jewelry.

"And something blue?"

When she wasn't looking, Sadie pointed one finger at the soft curls on Lollie's head.

Hannah snatched her older sister's wrist and scowled.

Pat laughed so hard, it woke her sleeping baby.

"I'm wearing something blue," April volunteered. "You just can't see it."

"Then let's go get married!" Moonie threw up his hands.

The party headed out the door.

April lingered only a moment before crossing the threshold to say a prayer. A prayer of thanksgiving for her family and her new home and her husband, and for darling Miss Cora who'd stopped her from sitting in her garden and eating worms on that fateful day.

The rest of the day went by in a blur. The vows, the reception line, the cake, the line of people throwing rice as she and Kurt ran down the walkway.

"You haven't told anyone that we're just going out to dinner right now and plan to come back to our house to spend our honeymoon, have you?" Kurt whispered in her ear just as they reached the car.

"Not a soul," she told him, planting a sly kiss on his smiling lips.

"Good." He kissed her back, full and wonderful and without a care for all the people cheering and hooting around them.

"Let's go." He opened the car door.

"The bouquet!" Hannah called out. "Throw the bouquet!"

April blinked, then just tossed it blindly—right into the hands of the closest female around. The one trying to get in one last word of advice to the newlyweds, even as they got in the car.

Kurt's mother!

And for the first time in the collective memory of Wileyville, Kentucky, Lollie Muldoon was speechless.

* * * * *

Dear Reader,

I began April's story with the idea of three sisters (Sadie's and Hannah's stories are told in *Sadie-in-Waiting* and *Mom Over Miami*) who, I hoped, represent, in part, the Christian women who faithfully serve their community, home and church, often without much recognition.

Through April I wanted to acknowledge the women on their own who sometimes take over when those with husbands, children or even elderly parents find themselves in a bind. Often it is assumed that single or widowed women without children at home have nothing else to do—and oh, how wrong that assumption can be!

The overall message of *April in Bloom* is that if we don't water our own garden it may begin to dry up and become unproductive. I wanted April to find love because that is what *she* wanted. For years she was someone who protected herself and her family, and when she no longer had to do that, it felt right that she blossom into her own person. After that—well, it was fun to give her a man who could benefit from the things she learned.

I hope you enjoy getting to know April and Kurt and the characters of Wileyville, Kentucky. If you want to read more about them and meet Sadie and Hannah, my Steeple Hill Café titles *Sadie-in-Waiting* and *Mom Over Miami* are available at retail outlets or from the bookstore at www.eHarlequin.com.

Blessings,

Annie Jones

QUESTIONS FOR DISCUSSION

1) In the story, Lollie Muldoon was the town gossip, and that negatively affected her son, Kurt. Do you think it's realistic that being the victim of gossip can cause long-term damage to people's view of themselves? Of others?

2) April felt responsible for protecting her younger sisters from the painful truth about their past but realized she had to let go of that responsibility in order to grow and find happiness. Do you believe people can make that kind of life-altering change any time in their lives? What makes it possible? What keeps them from doing it?

3) Would you ever want to live in a town like Wileyville where everyone knew you and your family and a lot about your life? Why or why not? Or if you live in such a town, what are the advantages and the drawbacks to it?

4) For fun, if you did live in Wileyville, what role would you want to play among the locals?

5) Miss Cora's father tried to create a self-sufficient town of only Christians. Do you think that was a good idea or destined to fail? Why?

6) The Council of Christian Women dedicated themselves to six weeks of service before Easter. Have you ever taken on a similar project? Would you ever want to try something like that?

7) Kurt planned to hide away from his problems by living in isolation. Do you think a man like Kurt could have actually stayed away from other people for long? If you had the chance, would you ever want to live in a secluded spot like Ezra's Holler?

8) April appreciated the correlation between Dogwood Winter and the promise of everlasting life. Do you draw inspiration for the evidence of God's love from everyday occurrences? Give an example.

*And now, turn the page for a sneak
preview of THE SISTERHOOD OF THE QUEEN
MAMAS by Annie Jones.*

*On sale in December 2006
from Steeple Hill Café.*

Chapter One

"Sisters, girlfriends and troublemakers (you know who you are), you are fearfully and wonderfully made! In other words, God doesn't make junk. Thankfully, his children do, and that's why we have been blessed with flea markets just about everywhere."

"The queen has spoken!"

"My name is Odessa Pepperdine, and I am *not* just some small-town silver-haired queen bee, my dears. I am the *queen mama of all queen bees* in the sweet little hive of friends I have made among the shoppers and shopkeepers at the Five Acres of Fabulous Finds Flea Market in Castle Rock, Texas. And it was on my say-so that we entitled this little bit here 'Chapter One.'"

"Even though, you'll soon discover, the *real* 'Chapter One' isn't actually going to start for a few more pages."

"That's Maxine Cooke-Nash, my sister in Christ and formerly—"

"Stranger in the community. That's what Odessa always says about us. Sisters in Christ, strangers in the community. We grew up living parallel lives on opposite sides of the proverbial tracks."

"What tracks?"

"I said *proverbial.* You know, just my delicate way of letting folks know that we stuck to opposite sides of town, you keeping company with people from your church, and me staying mostly within the African-American community."

"Only back then, when we were young, they didn't use that term *African-American.*"

"Oh, no, they didn't."

"They say you can never describe things in terms of black and white, but Maxine and I can tell you, if you were coming up in Castle Rock in the 1950s and '60s, well, you *could.*"

"Amen, Odessa. Amen."

"And coming up back then, Maxine and I were both active in the Campfire Girls, then went on to play high-school basketball, probably against each other more than once. Later, we both graduated top of our classes at Christian colleges, married ministers and settled down to raise our children, all within a few miles of each other. And we never met until we both tried to buy the same thing at the flea market."

"Are we telling this part *now?*"

"Oh. Oh, no. No, actually, we really *do* have something in mind in starting out things this way. As I said, I'm Odessa and this is Maxine—say hello properly, Maxine."

"Hi, y'all. Don't mind me. I may not say much, especially when Odessa is holding forth—and let's be upfront, when is she *not?* Anyway, I may not say much, but when I *do* speak up, I try to make it about something worthy of the effort."

"And she does. She *certainly* does, and this is the case with what she had to say about the way I wanted to begin to tell the story about what happened when... Well, there I'm getting ahead of myself."

"Which *she* does, and I have to rein her in."

"We're a good team like that, aren't we, Maxine?"

"Yes, we are. In fact, when it comes to reining in Odessa, I'm just about the only one who *can* anymore."

"I'm what people like to call irrepressible."

"Keep telling yourself that, Miss Pepperdine. And I'll keep tacking on that I've heard other words used to describe you."

"Oh, Maxine, you crack me up."

"Likewise, Odessa, honey."

"See, we *get* each other. We speak the same language, you might say. Though we did not start out on the best of terms at all. Oh, there now that reminds me! I was explaining about the way we decided to start our story."

"How?"

"You know, with Chapter One, the way you said, 'Uh, oh, let me tell this right.' *Maxine* said that whenever she sees a big bold heading like 'Foreword' or 'A Note from the Author' or sometimes even 'Prologue,' she tends to just skim right over it."

"I do. I'm sorry. But I think reading a book is a lot like eating a BLT sandwich—"

"Which is her favorite. My favorite used to be a nice simple chicken salad, but I like my food with a bolder flavor these days."

"Her chicken-salad days are behind her."

"And, oh, what happened to me at the flea market when… No, that's not what we were talking about. What was it, Maxine? Your love of a good BLT?"

"My love of a good book, actually, by way of my favorite sandwich, Odessa. See, often I think reading a book is a lot like a BLT sandwich on toast served up on my favorite lunch platter with chips and a pickle on the side. Done right, it *all* looks so good, but I'm anxious to sink my teeth in and get to the meat of it."

"But the meat of a book to one person might be nothing more than the olive stuck on a toothpick to hold the thing together to someone else, Maxine. So a book is not a sandwich."

"Well, a case *could* be made for that metaphor, Odessa. You know, with all the layers of story and setting and themes and—"

"No. I absolutely reject that analogy. If you have to compare a book to something edible and layered, you'd have to go with a hand-dipped chocolate truffle."

"One woman's chocolate is another woman's BLT. Now clink coffee cups with me so we can be in agreement and move on."

Clink.

"Anyway, when Maxine and I began this—"

"Ages and pages ago."

"Mumbling is not very *agreeable,* Maxine."

"Point taken."

Clink.

"We, Maxine and I, began this as 'Chapter One' because we are both ladies of a certain age who were brought up right."

"That dictates that we take a minute to introduce ourselves before we launch into our story."

"I mean, really, I wouldn't just walk up to a total stranger in the library and shout 'Call me Ishmael' or 'Scarlett O'Hara.' Would you, Maxine?"

"No, I would *not.* At least, not without offering them my hand, giving them my name and telling them why I wanted to say what I had to say to them."

"That's just good manners. And if Maxine and I are about *anything,* it's good manners."

"And using them to get our way."

Clink.

"Which is why you'll understand and hopefully forgive us for sticking 'Chapter One' on this part that might normally have said, you know, 'Foreword' or 'Prologue.'"

"Which is the part I usually skim over."

"And Maxine and I? Let me tell you, we are *not* women to be skimmed over!"

"Not anymore!"

"No, not anymore. Our days of being skimmed over are past us. We put in our time as mild-mannered ministers' wives and now have come to the days of speaking our minds and acting on the desires of our hearts!"

"*We* were mild-mannered but not our husbands. Just so there's no confusion. Because I can see where, at this point, you might find it hard to think of either Odessa or me as ever having been the kind most likely to inherit the earth."

"She means meek, for those of you who might not have picked up the Bible reference."

"Sermon on the mount."

"See? We really are ministers' wives."

"But not *mild-mannered* ministers, though they are both darling men in their own right."

"Oh, yes. Precious men. Smart and funny and Godly, both of them, and *men* through and through."

"Which is why, once they retired, Odessa and I started going to the flea market, to escape from—"

"Find respite."

"Find respite for a few hours each week from our retired hubbies."

"Oh, and to try to collect the one thing we both wanted with all our worldly beings for ourselves—"

"Ever since we were both young—and, please note, I do mean *young*—brides in the 1960s…"

"The entire twenty-piece line of chip-proof kitchenware made by the Royal Service Company of Akron, Ohio, the black-and-gold-on-white 'Hostess Queen' pattern."

Clink.

"Anyway, we just wanted to introduce ourselves and this BLT of a story—"

"Truffle."

"That we have to share and why we have to share it."

"You see, Maxine and me weren't always queen mamas."

"No, we were not."

"Or queen bees."

"Worker bees, more like it."

"Regular drones."

"Which isn't a bad thing. Now, don't get Odessa wrong there but—"

"But the time comes when even a drone has to stop and look around and say 'It's time to create a buzz.'"

"And oh, what a buzz Odessa made!"

"I did. Though I didn't do it just for myself. That I want made clear right from the start. I did it for all of us."

"The drones—"

"And the meek—"

"And the women who are strangers in their own communities—"

"Who are all wonderfully and fearfully made."
Clink.

"There's your meat of the story, Maxine, right there."

"Shh. You're getting ahead again when all we wanted to do with this introduction part... That's what we could have called it, the 'Introduction.'"

"And you're telling me you wouldn't have skimmed something called the 'Introduction'?"

"Well, no, I *am* a skimmer, I do confess."

"Right, and if we got other skimmers in the crowd and they went into the story and suddenly you or I popped in with a comment—"

"Have you ever heard that expression *a month of Sundays?*"

"What now, Odessa?"

"I was just thinking about how the story of when we first all got thrown together until the *incident* was just about a month of flea markets."

"You mean the span of four flea markets?"

No, I mean... Let me see, from July fourth until Labor Day, weekly flea markets, lasting three days—except we never come out on Sundays, being the Lord's day—but you can count it because some things happened on Sundays. So that means—"

"Hold on. Odessa is trying to do the math in her head. This could take a minute."

"Got it. Three days a week over about nine weeks, plus extra for Labor Day weekend, makes twenty-eight days, so that's right. About a month of flea markets from start to finish to tell the story of how our new friends Jan, Bernadette and Chloe—"

"Ahem."

"Oh, right, don't want to give too much away."

"Let's just say it involves some collectible kitsch and some baked goods."

"Oh, and don't forget to mention—"

"The tiaras. The story is just jam-packed with tiaras."

"Hey, Maxine and I can tell you, a woman wears a lot of hats in her lifetime—why shouldn't one of them be a crown?"

Clink.

"And also a hot-air balloon."

"I got nothing for that one."

"You, Odessa?"

"Oh, wait, yes I do."

"More like it."

"Up, up and away!"

"See y'all in a page or two and don't forget…"

"Stay queenly!"